CW01080350

Nirmal Babu's Bride

INDIALOG PUBLICATIONS PVT. LTD.

Nirmal Babu's Bride

ALISON MUKHERJEE

INDIALOG PUBLICATIONS PVT. LTD.

Published by

Indialog Publications Pvt. Ltd.
O - 22, Lajpat Nagar II
New Delhi - 110024
Ph.: 91-11-6839936/6320504
Fax: 91-11-6935221
Internet Addresses: http://www.indialogpublications.com
                    http://www.onepageclassic.com

First Published June 2002.
Copyright © Alison Mukherjee

Printed at Chaman Enterprises, Darya Ganj, New Delhi

ISBN 81-87981-23-7

For Gomer,
daughter of Diblaim,
whose story is told in the book
of the prophet Hosea

CHAPTER ONE

1999

∽◯◯∽

Sunil turns to look at his youngest sister Rupa, who is sitting in the back of the taxi, and although she meets his eyes with a smile, there is exhaustion in her face – eyebrows drawn downwards and a tightness about her lips. He's finding it difficult to keep up a conversation as they drive the hour and a half from Calcutta Airport because of the harsh noise of the engine, the uneven road surface which demands attention if you are to avoid being thrown about, him being in the front with her in the back so he has to twist his neck round before speaking, her words escaping through the open window.... Although she replies to him she doesn't push the conversation forward, so he is doing more of the talking than she is. He apologizes for the holes in the road and explains that the contractors who mend them use poor quality materials, and that in future the government plans to force them to guarantee their work. He points out men who crouch beside large containers, constantly agitating the surface of the water with their hands, and tells her these contain newly hatched fish which will die unless the water is kept aerated.

As he stood in the sun outside the "Arrivals" building and peered into the dim interior, Sunil thought he could see her struggling to take her suitcase off the revolving track. Then as she wheeled the luggage trolley out into the light, searching the crowd of faces with eyes narrowed against the brightness, he was sure. She came smiling

9

towards him, her small neat figure more elegant and confident than when she last visited, let him kiss her cheeks, and said how happy she was to have finally arrived. They were relieved to recognize each other, yet there was a reserve on her part for which he was unprepared. He had imagined this meeting many times while he waited, supplying the emotional detail, her happy tears, his warm comfort, but he hadn't allowed for the intervening years.

When she first visited ten years ago, Rupa charmed them all with her enthusiasm. Crouching in front of the pump, self-conscious but determined, as Sunil's wife patiently showed her how to wash her own clothes, how to rub the block of turmeric colored soap across the dirtiest patches. Learning which bits of kitchen waste the hens would eat and where they laid their eggs, accompanying Sunil's little daughter as she called them in at night *"ai ai ai ai ai ti ti ti ti tee!"* Now Rupa is much older, a graduate with a responsible job, obviously she's changed.

A double garland of pink and yellow plastic flowers hangs in the front windscreen, swaying drunkenly from side to side as the vehicle lurches forward. Partially obscured by the lurid flowers, Rupa notices a small statue of Ganesh fixed to the dashboard surrounded by tiny flashing lights.

"My sister," Sunil informs the taxi driver, "a wealthy and most important lady. She's come to visit us."

The driver slumps sideways, his shoulder pressed against the door. He sounds the horn repeatedly with his thumb, depressing the switch situated conveniently on the rim of the steering wheel where he can reach it without shifting his grip. "From America?" he asks in a respectful tone.

"England."

"Oh, so she lives in London! My second cousin brother's neighbor has been to London." The driver glances briefly at his back-seat passenger, more relaxed now that he feels she's not a complete stranger.

"Not London, she lives in England but not in London. There are other cities in England, didn't you know?" Sunil is about to expand on this theme so Rupa leaves them to their conversation. In any case she finds the driver's way of speaking difficult to follow.

She too has played this arrival scene many times in her head but it won't go smoothly, she can't get it quite right. It's not as straightforward as last time when she was thrilled just to discover these relatives and widen the boundary of her family beyond the confines of mother and daughter. This time it's bound to be different because she knows just being with them is not enough, she wants to speak with her family about things which Ma never speaks of, at home. Rupa has always known she has a brother and a sister somewhere in India, but Ma has never supplied an explanation to why the family lives apart.

This time Rupa is determined to ask questions, yet she's not quite comfortable with the plan, it strikes her as deceptive, slightly dishonest. It means she's coming not only as one of the family but also as an investigator, one who might disturb lives that have been carefully constructed. These doubts leave her feeling irritable and vaguely depressed. This mood is partly due to tiredness and nerves, it will soon burn off like morning fog. She tells herself to make an effort, try instead to concentrate on the excitement, the joy of being here again.

With hungry concentration Rupa watches everything they pass on the road, eyes screwed up against the dust which blows through the half open window, one hand restraining her frenzied hair. Young men carrying expressionless girls on the crossbars of their cycles, garrulous men sitting at tea shops, noisy and garish advertisements, fish farms and fields of green crops, half-finished mansions, a whole family on a single scooter, crowded buses with passengers protruding from every orifice, blaring lorries charging at everything in their path, laborers squatting at the roadside, children squabbling, married women wearing cheap bright saris and boasting a wide stripe of vermilion in the partings of their hair.

"You know, Sunil dada, it's so good to be here again," Rupa says with conviction. "Thank you for letting me come."

"It's good to have you here, thank you for coming." Sunil replies with mock formality, laughing at her politeness. "What is this, 'thank you' to your own brother?" he teases. "'Please', 'thank you', 'sorry' all day long, that's how the English talk, but is it from the heart? That's what I want to know."

"Mine was, honestly!" she insists, and joins in his laughter. He treats her like a little sister, so that's what she'll be.

From behind Rupa can see the shiny skin of Sunil's scalp. His wavy hair is thinning on top and even the tiny coils on his neck are flecked with gray. She reflects that everything about him, his full cheeks, round figure, soft voice, is reassuring and conveys kindness, that he would have been a good older brother to grow up with. She tries to imagine it, herself as a young child hanging round Sunil and his gang of friends, but the scene remains a blur because she fails to decide on the location. He won't fit into the streets where she spent her childhood, and she can't see herself growing up in West Bengal, in these surroundings.

Field after field of straw colored crops stretches away from the road, interspersed with squares of fresh green. The sawed trunks of mature trees lie in rows on the verges, their flesh dull reddish-brown. The taxi approaches a junction and is brought to a halt by a khaki figure standing in the middle of the road. One hand holds a lathi with which he administers a restraining tap to the bonnet of a jeep in the manner of a lion-tamer, in the other is an umbrella which shades him from the sun. Despite this show of authority, it seems to Rupa that the real decisions about which vehicle will move off first are negotiated by the drivers themselves, via nods and hand gestures.

The taxi leaves the highway and turns down a narrow lane. the surface is still tarmac but so broken up that it's hardly recognizable as such. A girl pours water over her younger brother as he crouches laughing under the roadside tap. In a front open workshop a sweating boy grips one end of the iron girder, struggling to keep its other end in the center of the furnace while his father hammers it into shape.

The taxi turns into an even narrower lane composed of bricks laid tightly side by side. Rupa notices a heap of sandals piled outside a hut designated "Youth Club." Through the doorway she glimpses a live television screen and rows of benches. Brushed by hedges and low branches on both sides, the taxi now moves more slowly, beneath the tyres bricks have given way to clay. Thatched round stacks of rice straw, and ruminating cattle, occupy the yards in front of houses set back from the lane, witness to the recent change in land use from agriculture to residential.

"We're almost there," Sunil turns and smiles encouragingly. "The children will be watching out for us, they're so excited. Specially Priya, she couldn't sleep last night. Her friends, even her teachers, know you're arriving today."

He tells the driver to stop by the next house, and invites him in to take some refreshment before the return journey. The driver declines the offer and they haggle briefly over the fare. Rupa chases off that moment of reluctance, the lethargy that prefers to go on traveling than to arrive, and gathers her hand luggage. Sliding stickily across the rexine seat, she opens the heavy door and climbs out onto the hard-packed earth. Sunil cheerfully drags her suitcase from the boot.

Chhaya, Sunil's wife, comes smiling down the veranda steps, her elbows pointing upwards as she hurriedly knots her hair on top of her head. With two fingers she lifts Rupa's chin, and kisses both her cheeks, her hand momentarily lingering to stroke the tired skin.

"You look worn out." Chhaya is thin without being angular, her body is both soft and strong. Although she couldn't be described as good-looking, her long face has no particular sweetness of its own, her serene expression's everything.

"Tired, yes, but I'll soon recover."

"Did they feed you properly on the plane or are you hungry?" Chhaya carries Rupa's hand luggage up the steps and, having first spread out a sheet of newspaper, places the bag carefully on the floor beside the iron bed which occupies one end of the veranda. She does everything carefully. If she lived in England, Chhaya would follow a recipe meticulously and faithfully obey laundry instructions on clothing labels. Because her mother told her a woman's hair should be tightly bound at night, she carefully braids hers before sleeping, right up to the last few wispy strands. Chhaya's presence is reassuring, she's predictable and safe.

"They gave us too much to eat, Chhaya boudi, I don't need anything more. Really." As she enters the shade of the veranda Rupa is aware her breathing slows down and the ache across her shoulders fades away. "Just a glass of water." She smiles at Chhaya and reaches out affectionately to take her hand. They both turn to watch Sunil as he eagerly follows them up the steps, straining against the weight of the suitcase. Coming home to this place, to these people, he is like a musician unclipping the back of his harmonium, beginning to work the bellows and press the keys as he prepares to perform his favorite song.

"Water first, of course, but after that let's have some tea. They may have fed you lots on the plane but what kind of food was it, that's the important question." Sunil drops Rupa's suitcase on its side, grabs the towel which is dangling from a wire stretched across the veranda grills, and with it rubs his forehead and the back of his neck.

"What do you expect, are they going to serve food as good as you eat in your house? No chance." Rupa laughs.

"Your brother thinks too much about food, I've told him he needs to cut down, take care of his heart." Chhaya frowns a warning at her husband before disappearing behind the length of printed cloth which hangs across the kitchen doorway.

Sunil waves his hand as if to brush aside her cautionary remark, then throws the towel onto the bed. He nods proudly towards the girl who is sitting there, her legs jiggling in embarrassment, her shining eyes fixed on their visitor. "Look, Rupa, would you have recognized Priya?"

Rupa shakes her head in surprise and sits down beside her niece. Priya squirms her shoulders and giggles self-consciously as Rupa comments on how grown-up she looks, and asks how she's getting on at school. Rupa tries to recall the chubby three year old of ten years ago, who chattered endlessly, and sang and danced her own creations with such joyful energy for anyone she could persuade to watch. Priya would sit naked on a low stool in the sunshine while her mother crouched beside her, rubbing the child's soft skin with mustard oil before bathing her like a pampered princess on a throne graciously suffering the ministrations of her maidservant. Rupa often took her out for walks – each one a new adventure for this was something Priya had not done before. She walked to Church, to the ricksha stand, to the corner shop, but she never walked just for the sake of walking. She would carry on a conversation with the neighbors as she passed by.

"So, Priya, where're you off to now?"

"I'm going to find a husband," breathlessly as her plump legs hurried to keep up with Rupa's longer ones.

"Where will you find a good boy? Tell me that."

"Oh, I'll easily find three or four to marry me."

"Surely one's more than enough!" By which time she'd moved forwards to another conversation. Rupa remembers thinking, this child has no doubt about her own significance.

Quickly losing her adolescent shyness, Priya asks about the plane journey and listens to the answers with dramatic expressions of amazement and delight, such a rewarding audience that Rupa is tempted to exaggerate a little for the sake of the response. She talks of limitless supplies of sweets and toys bestowed on young passengers by air hostesses each one as beautiful as a film star, and claims the plane with its gorgeous wallpaper and satin cushions was as luxurious as the grandest of hotels. Then Rupa describes how, when the sky flushed bright pink above the purple mass of cloud at sunset, the wings of the plane blushed a pink response for a few moments before fading to dull gray. And how, in defiance of instructions to keep the window shutters closed, she had peeped out at midnight and seen gold dust, pearls and silver sequins embroidered on the black velvet of the desert. Priya is enchanted.

Sunil, now wearing only vest and lungi, emerges from one of the two rooms which open off the veranda. He nods approvingly in their direction as he hurries into the kitchen to see if the tea's ready and to remind Chhaya to make Rupa's separately without sugar, before bustling back again.

"Where's your little brother, Priya? Where's he gone?" Sunil wants everyone there to welcome her, to make sure there's nothing lacking in their hospitality. Rupa's eyes meet Priya's and they share a thought, he doesn't need to fuss so much, everything's fine.

Chhaya carries in a tray of cups and biscuits. "He's not here." She pronounces the words with artificial precision. "I don't know where he's got to. Perhaps he's playing with his friends." With her eyes she indicates the place where Bijoy is hiding just inside the doorway, listening to every word but not ready yet to risk an appearance. By flattening himself against the wall he can peep between the door frame and the curtain, so that all he can see of Rupa is a long plain gray skirt and one foot, the toenails of which are painted with navy polish.

"I've some surprises for him in my suitcase." Rupa's comment is directed temptingly at the doorway.

For a while they sit together and talk, re-spinning the web that has torn and grown slack because of distance and the passage of time. Rupa is absorbed by their simple intimacy and she offers no resistance, listening to the details of their daily lives and responding to the many queries they have about hers. What does she eat for breakfast, wear to work, watch on TV? Where does she live, shop, go on holiday? When her limited vocabulary lets her down they help her out, suggesting words and puzzling over the descriptions she makes with her hands. Priya fetches a pencil and paper for illustrations.

Rupa thinks, this is how it should be, these people who are tied to you by more than friendship. Chhaya has the rare ability to make you feel she's really attending to you, only to you, when you're speaking. Her responses are calm and measured, a natural counselor. Sunil's the entertainer. He tells them of a friend who, on his first visit to Delhi, proudly ordered his meal in English – "Bring me kitchen curry and fire rice!" And mimics Chhaya's expressions of despair the day her bag was stolen as they returned together by train from her sister's wedding. Sunil waited until they were safely home before showing his wife her gold ornaments, still safe where he'd concealed them in the secret pocket in his waistband. His comic anecdotes and gentle teasing flavor their conversation.

As they talk, a little boy emerges limb by limb from his hiding place and hovers in the doorway, his hostile stare fixed on Rupa. "Why has she got short hair? She's a lady isn't she?" Bijoy asks, addressing his question to the curtain which he's twisted round and round until it's transformed into a thick cable. Priya gasps at his rudeness and buries her face in the towel earlier discarded by her father.

"People in England think it looks pretty that way," Chhaya explains. "You've seen fashion shows on the television, remember? The models have all kinds of hairstyles."

"You know, Bijoy, it's much quicker to comb short hair, that's why I have mine cut like this. I don't like getting up in the mornings, so I'd be late for work if I had to spend a long time on my hair." Rupa nudges Priya to reassure her that her brother's bluntness hasn't caused offence. "Whose hair takes the most time in your house, yours or Priya's? See what I mean?" she continues. Bijoy frowns and winds the curtain even tighter.

But there are no questions about Ma, who after all is Sunil's mother too. Rupa wonders if he feels the weight of those absent questions as she does. It seems to her that Ma is there on the veranda with them, but they're ignoring her, pretending she's invisible. Whereas Rupa perceives everything twice, once for herself and then again through Ma's eyes, as she has done since she was a child.

Eventually Chhaya stands up with the tray, ready to go back into the kitchen to prepare the evening meal. She suggests Rupa go upstairs to see the room where she'll be sleeping, and Rupa knows from the way Chhaya's eyes scan the hem of her skirt and hover round her hands and neckline, what she really means is Rupa should bathe and change her clothes. That the outside dirt, the contamination from plane and airport and taxi, must be removed from her person. Rupa is happy to oblige.

When Rupa visited before, the house was newly built, the floors were of rough brick, the walls unplastered, and there was no electricity. That was part of the adventure, evenings by hurricane lamp, nothing but scratchy hand fans with which to produce a cooling draught and keep off the mosquitoes. Now Rupa can see how much the house has changed and their lives improved. The veranda floor is polished red with a black geometrical design set in the center, the walls are covered in green lime-wash and each room has a blue formica box containing switches and sockets. She looks up to see fluorescent lights and ceiling fans. Priya proudly leads Rupa up the concrete stairs sheltered by corrugated iron sheets, which run outside the house. Half way up they pass a hen snuggled down inside a wide flat bowl which has been placed on a stool. As they pass, the hen moves its head sideways to get a better look at them but decides she's not in any danger. Priya laughs.

"She sits there all day, but she's so stupid! When she wants to lay, she moves onto the stairs and the egg breaks as it rolls down."

Rupa pushes open the bathroom door and enters the hollow dampness. Concrete, metal, porcelain, no fluffy towels or furry bath mats. A wire stretches across the corner of the room and she hangs her clean clothes over this before undressing, feeling more starkly naked amid these hard surfaces than in the comfort of her bathroom back home. Someone has carried up two buckets of water to await her arrival. The mug knocks against the iron bucket as she fills it, producing a wet echo. Her stomach muscles contract and nipples harden as she pours cool water over her body, again and again, enjoying the freedom of splashing water carelessly onto the floor. Tingling with renewed energy, she dries herself vigorously with a thin gamchha supplied by Chhaya, and puts on crumpled cotton clothes straight from the suitcase. Long and loose so as not to cause offence.

As she's about to leave the bathroom she catches sight of her face in a mirror hanging on a hook near the door. Spots and streaks speckle the glass but she can clearly see her own eyes staring back. Not the perfect ovals of a classic beauty, Rupa's eyes are hazelnuts rather than almonds. As a child this gave her a startled look, as if she was permanently trapped in the dazzle of car headlights. Now her eyes are thoughtful, deep round pools, too dark to fathom. Nor does her face boast sculptured cheekbones or a clearly defined jaw, in fact her forehead is the only place where her skull is visible beneath the skin, everywhere else the bone is generously rounded out with flesh. She turns sideways in an attempt to see the back of her head, to imagine what her shaggy haircut looks like to someone who sees only women with long oiled locks, rippling free or bound in buns and plaits. She notices her nose, small and round, and smiles as she recalls how when she was very young Ma used to make fun of it and, dipping her fingers into baby oil, pretend to squeeze the tip into a point each night before Rupa slept.

Having bathed and changed her clothes she climbs the narrow stairs onto the roof from where she can see other roofs, rafts floating in the surrounding sea of leaves. Some are unfinished and covered with plastic sheets weighed down with bricks. Next door the roof is hung with a line of long petticoats and three-cornered nappies stitched from torn saris, and on a roof further away someone has molded little black balls and laid them in rows to dry, a mixture of coal dust and starch, fuel for the oven. To the front lie two open fields, before more trees rise up and flow into the distance. Up here a light breeze blows, and leaves stir on all sides. The view fills her with the greenness of well-being, spiced with anticipation.

"Pishi, Rupa pishi!" Priya calls out with a note of urgency in her voice. "My dad says aren't you going to come down and meet Dadu? He's just come back." Priya runs barefoot up the steps to stand beside Rupa on the roof. Bijoy trails solemnly a few paces behind. Together they look out over the low wall which runs round the edge of the roof, resting their elbows on the rough brick. Rupa recognizes some of the trees from her last visit; the absurdly large sal leaves under which a whole family could shelter from the sun or rain, the feathery parallel leaves of the graceful sojne, the sturdy and reliable mango with its narrow glossy leaves arranged in a series of rosettes, at first sight not so different from the upward facing rounder leaves of the jackfruit. And lower down she can see papaya fruits hang heavily from a scarred trunk, the leaves cut out like children's paper patterns stuck on the windows of a primary school classroom. Banana leaves thrust straight up trying to break through the other foliage but in vain because they are too short, while palms fountain out meekly in a circle. Betel nut trees laden with bright orange fruits look to Rupa like sentries standing in a row along the boundary of the property, their stiff punk hair styles contrasting with the dreadlocks which hang right over the faces of coconut palms.

Priya points out the distant subabul trees with their dark

hanging pods, and explains that they belong to Doctor babu who planted them in a piece of land he bought but will soon sell, to pay for his brother's marriage. Then Bijoy shows Rupa the recently installed television aerial, the field where he flies his kite, and the house where his friend lives.

"Come on Rupa pishi, Dadu's waiting." Bijoy's voice is unlike a child's voice, rather hoarse and rough.

CHAPTER TWO

When she was very young Rupa hardly noticed that she didn't have a father. If teachers wanted her to write about home, or draw pictures of her family, she just invented a second parent. It was fun deciding which figure to choose, once she drew a smiling face sitting in a bus, once a tall thin man resting his elbows on the counter in a shop, but it was never more than that, a drawing on a piece of school paper. She and Ma were complete, there was no father-shaped gap in their lives, she didn't miss her father any more than she missed having a swimming-pool in the garden or going to California on holiday.

She had assumed when she first visited Bengal that the biological bond guaranteed an emotional response, and with her brother and sister this was true, but when Rupa met her father, nothing happened. No upsurge of daughterly love. On the contrary, she felt repugnance. He irritated her with his self-righteousness, drawing her attention to his generosity (clothes for the maidservant's children, medicine for the rickshavala's mother), and with his constant criticisms of the neighbors whom, nevertheless, he needed to impress. By the end of four weeks, Rupa was finding it difficult to control her voice when she replied to his questions, hard to avoid any hint of the distaste she felt for him. On reflection later, another explanation occurred to her; perhaps she had decided subconsciously, even before meeting Nirmal babu, that growing fond of him would be a betrayal of Ma's love. She knew it was common for children to feel torn between separated parents, to bestow all their loyalty on one or the other. Rupa was devoted to her mother, it was obvious who she'd choose. She hadn't given her father a fair chance.

She tells herself that in view of her increased age and wider life experience, things should be easier this time. But emotion is no great respecter of reason, and as she anticipates seeing him again her limbs flood with acid and her bones crumble. With one hand resting on Bijoy's shoulder and the other looped through Priya's arm, Rupa descends the stairs. The children's presence affords her extra courage.

Nirmal babu is sitting on his deck chair in the veranda, his crossed legs so thin that both feet rest flat on the floor. His shirt and trousers are faded, frayed at hem, cuffs and collar. Rupa stoops to take the dust of his feet, as he'd insisted she learn how to do, and his hand rests momentarily on her head in a gesture of blessing. She is uncomfortably aware of the deep cracks around his heels, of the excessive hair in his ears and nostrils, of the acrid smell of cigarette smoke which his body emits, and of his few remaining discolored teeth. She still feels no tenderness towards this man who is her father and has to admit that nothing's changed, except that this time he is a key witness in her investigation, albeit one who will never agree to testify.

He asks when she left England, how long the journey took, if she is tired, the kind of questions neighbors routinely ask. Rupa's replies are as brief and bland as his questions, fortunately she can escape by assuming the demeanor required of a young person towards her elders. She is conscious this is cowardly, a way of avoiding real conversation, but in his presence nothing else seems possible. Nirmal babu has the hollow dignity of one who expects to be respected, but whose expectation knows nothing of earning or deserving respect. Rupa has sat in meetings where embarrassed young managers have allowed men like her father to speak at length, out of a desire to appear courteous, but with no intention of taking their words seriously. She wishes she could feel sympathy – pity at least – but can't.

"You've come at the right time. The weather during this month of Kartik is rather pleasant – not very hot during daytime nor too cold at night. I told them not to let you come in the summer, you wouldn't survive the heat – and the rainy season, it's unbearably humid then. You'd be ill, catch a fever, not be able to enjoy your holiday. This season's definitely the best." He speaks attentively but without enthusiasm, seems uneasy and does not meet her eye. And then Rupa realizes what is wrong – he too can see Ma with them on the veranda. In fact all he can see is Ma, who has deliberately placed herself between him and his youngest daughter.

Sunil stands uncertainly in the kitchen doorway trying to concentrate on the bazaar instructions Chhaya is giving, but also anxious to supervise the meeting between Rupa and her father. Sunil was relieved to see Rupa relax as they talked together earlier, and then to hear her laughter mingle with the children's on the roof. Now sitting there opposite Baba she has tightened up again, her shoulders twist awkwardly as she turns her face away. Baba keeps staring at her, bewildered, his fingers kneading his palms as if to mold the right words.

"You'd never guess, would you Rupa, that he's seventy-four? Doctor babu says he'll last another twenty years at least!" Sunil is unsure of how best to intervene. He knows they are both uncomfortable and feels responsible, as he's felt responsible all his life. Responsible, when his mother went away, for tying his sister's hair in two red-ribboned bunches and setting her on the crossbar of his cycle so he could transport her to school; for standing in line with the ration cards to collect their allocation of rice and wheat, sugar and kerosene; for reminding his father to pay the maidservant's wages.

When his wife disappeared Nirmal babu became more and more absorbed in school affairs, leaving him with little energy to attend to the business of running a household. Sunil, in spite of his youth, filled the gap, tried also to bring some laughter into their dreary lives. In his mother's absence it fell to Sunil to keep the peace between a father, preoccupied and grumpy, and a sister, stubborn and contrary. The demands made upon him when still

23

young have shaped his character, which means so long as Rupa stays in his house Sunil will do his best to safeguard her happiness.

From the lane a voice calls, repeating the word in rising crescendos – "dudh, dudh," – and a figure wheels a cycle in through the gate. Having propped his cycle against the mango tree in the garden, the rider detaches a small churn from behind the seat and prepares to dispense milk into a measuring cup. Chhaya comes out from the kitchen carrying a strainer and a stainless steel bowl.

"I'll need an extra cup this evening, and every day for the next three weeks. Can you manage that?" she inquires as he pours the liquid through the strainer into her bowl.

"Of course he can manage, all he has to do is add more water!" Sunil jokes. "You'll have to use boiled water from now on, dudhvala, we have a visitor from England who isn't used to our Bengali germs."

The distraction allows Nirmal babu to retreat to his room, mumbling that it's time to listen to the news. Soon, amidst crackle and whine, distorted voices swell and fade as national and local politics, weather and sport are disgorged into his room. The sound forms a defensive shield around him, and leaves Rupa dry with disappointment.

Chhaya declines an offer of help in the kitchen – later maybe but not on her first day – and Sunil's gone to the bazaar, so Rupa wanders into the room where Priya and Bijoy are studying. Bijoy bends over an exercise book in which he's writing heavily with a pencil, reciting as he writes, totally engrossed in his work. Around him on the floor lie his open school box and a variety of text books. From the bed Priya watches as Rupa enters, then pretends to concentrate on her books, sighing as she restlessly turns pages and rearranges piles of papers. Not wanting to disturb their study, Rupa picks up a collection of sample English exam questions, and is first amused and then troubled by the unfamiliar language.

Her attention is drawn to four geckos on the wall, she watches as they turn their heads lazily this way and that, surrounded by insects they have no need to move in order to feed. Insects tiny and round, long and green, bright and shiny, whir round in circles, crawl up the wall slowly in straight lines, scuttle crazily in zigzag patterns. Rupa has prepared herself for creepy crawlies and won't make a fuss. A moth blunders into the strip light and flaps around below it. The geckos are suddenly tense, each cautiously attempts to stalk the moth as it moves unpredictably between air space and the hard wall surface. The moth lands just beside the smallest one which snaps it up instantly and scurries off to consume it beneath the window. The three larger geckos look confused, offended, and when the smaller one returns to the group they chase it aggressively, as if in punishment for not abiding by the natural hierarchy.

"There are always masses of insects, all kinds of insects, around Kali Puja time. Sometimes we catch them and feed them to the hens for protein, but most of them get burned up in the candles and oil lamps. Baba says that's the real reason for having Kali Puja, because there are too many insects." Priya is watching Rupa watch the geckos.

"Kali Puja?"

"You don't know Kali Puja? It comes after Durga Puja which is really the big festival. People are making pandals now all round the town. They're not as good as the Durga Puja pandals, but we've got one by our riksha stand on the crossroads. Later they'll put images of Kali inside and play the mike very loud and everyone'll come to see." Priya's eyes widen and her eyebrows rise in excitement, then glancing towards Nirmal babu's door she lowers her voice. "Dadu doesn't let us go out on Kali Puja night because people get drunk and do things they shouldn't. They do really disgusting things, you can't imagine. He doesn't like us looking at the pandals at all, well he doesn't mind too much about the pandals but when the images are inside we aren't allowed to look."

"Perhaps he'll let you come with me if I say I want to see them?" Rupa tries to guess what response Priya expects from her. "We can take photos to show people in England." *And photos of you and your brother to break your grandmother's heart. She will never see your shining eyes, touch your brother's curls, or hear you talk of subabul trees and stupid hens. Let her at least have photos of you.* Of course Rupa could never actually show Ma the photos, for her the children don't exist.

"He won't let us. He won't, he won't." Priya closes her eyes, turns down the corners of her mouth and waggles her head from side to side. Bijoy has stopped writing and, eyes fixed on his sister's face, is holding his breath. "He won't!" he whispers in agreement. The curtain covering the kitchen doorway is pulled to one side and Chhaya comes through, shaking her head in warning, one finger pressed to her lips.

"They have to study every night and again early in the morning, otherwise they'd never cover the syllabus. It's vast." Chhaya sits down on the mat beside Bijoy, while she talks she checks through the work he's been doing, jabbing at the page with her finger as she points out his mistakes.

"I hope you don't feel bored? Your sister should be back from school soon. She had to go, you understand, it was an important meeting. She couldn't get out of it."

"No, no I'm fine, Chhaya boudi, honestly. I'm very happy just sitting here and listening and smelling and watching everything, remembering what this life's like." Rupa interlocks her fingers and stretches her arms above her head, a satisfied shiver passes through her. "My internal clock's all jumbled up anyway, it'll take a day or two before it settles down."

"What do you want to do while you're here? We could take a picnic, hire a van, and all go out for the day, to the Calcutta Zoo, or Nabadwip?" Chhaya looks at her children to catch the excitement in their faces before turning to Rupa again. "Is there anywhere you'd specially like to go?"

"I'll need to consult with Priya madam and Bijoy babu. We'll let you know tomorrow." Rupa winks at the children who look disconcerted, uncertain how their mother will respond to this play-acting.

Rupa wants to tell Chhaya she's interested in finding out about Ma's background and uncovering the reasons for her escape to England, but she can't do that in front of the children. Perhaps she couldn't confide in Chhaya anyway, considering she's so reluctant to allow discussion of anything contentious. But Ma, of course, can go one better, she can deflect a question without even acknowledging it has been asked. Rupa remembers one occasion when she tried to ask her mother directly about the past. Ma had a way of continuing on undisturbed right through what she was saying, so that when Rupa finished making her tentative enquiry, Ma came out the other side still busy kneading dough for the rootis. And then she flattened Rupa's words along with the rolled out balls of dough. Rupa gave up after that, deciding to accept defeat.

And then quite unexpectedly on Rupa's eighteenth birthday, Ma suggested she visit India between 'A' levels and going to university, for a month or so. If she wanted to, that is, if she was interested in seeing the country where her mother grew up. Rupa, puzzled by the suddenness of this proposal, replied that she was definitely interested, and held her breath in case Ma changed her mind again. Sufficient money was withdrawn from the building society, and when Rupa's exams finished, Ma handed over the tickets and some cash to spend during the trip. Once she was with the family in Bengal, Rupa readily accepted that some things were never mentioned here either. After all, she was accustomed to the same selective silences at home.

Later that evening Rupa's elder sister, Jayanti, arrives back home after her meeting. She comes round the corner of the house still complaining about the rickshavala whom she accuses of charging more than the correct fare. Having wearily ascended the veranda steps, she collapses onto the iron bed, slipping the strap of her cloth bag off her shoulder.

"Priya, Priya! What's keeping you so busy? Your pishima's come home, have you forgotten her glass of water?"

"I'm coming, Jayanti pishi! Wait a minute, I'm coming." Priya appears from the room where's she's been studying, and hurries into the kitchen. Jayanti watches her with stern approval.

"Where's Bijoy got to? What about my books, are they going to stay here all night?" Bijoy comes out of his grandfather's room and, conscious that his is an important task, carries Jayanti's bag into the other room.

Rupa's enthusiastic greeting is acknowledged with a brusque nod and instructions to follow her sister upstairs so that they can talk while Jayanti changes her clothes. Rupa slides gracefully into the obedient younger sister role, although she's had few rehearsals. She climbs the stairs to Jayanti's room and stretches out on the bed, flat on her back, ankles crossed, fingers interlocked across her chest, while her sister is busy changing. From her prone position Rupa can see the ceiling fan, dark green picked out in gold, more classy than anything in the downstairs rooms. The window grills up here are an intricate design of loops and curls whereas the downstairs windows are protected by parallel bars. The yellow walls have been newly painted and Rupa wonders if this is in her honor.

"This one for a staff meeting?" She reaches out to feel the fabric of the discarded sari thrown casually onto the bed, rubbing it between forefinger and thumb.

Jayanti looks up from making the pleats of her house-wearing sari and shrugs, "Everyone wears silk nowadays. A decent sari means a silk one. You can't find those synthetic ones any more, or not good ones anyway, only the sort maidservants wear."

Working behind the screen of the cotton sari draped across her, Jayanti unhooks the opening at the front of her blouse and eases it off her shoulders, then runs her forefinger under the tight sleeves where they cut into the soft flesh of her upper arms, loosening them before pulling the garment right off. She lets the worn blouse fall to the floor and Rupa passes her a clean one.

"What does it feel like then, Rupa, being back here with us again? Last time you loved it so much that you didn't want to leave. Remember?"

Rupa watches, fascinated. Jayanti's figure, hanging breasts, prominent stomach, thick waist, broad yet flat hips so that in side view the bulge in front is greater than the one behind, and her heavy deliberate movements, are so familiar, so much like Ma's.

"You must have noticed how much everything's changed? This room for instance, it was built quite recently, three years ago. And the one next to it, where you'll be sleeping, that was only added last summer." Jayanti doesn't expect a response, she's concentrating on what she's doing, continuing to talk in order to keep the initiative in this reunion with her little sister. "No doubt we too have changed, though we don't notice it." She's slightly unsettled to see that Rupa is not in fact such a little sister any more. Her confidence and maturity have taken Jayanti by surprise.

Jayanti looks up momentarily and frowns at Rupa. "You've lost weight. Nothing's wrong is it? You're not ill or anything?"

"I'm fine!" Rupa's reply is almost defensive. There's no tender concern in Jayanti's question, it's more like an accusation.

When she has finished dressing Jayanti arranges herself purposefully on the bed next to Rupa. She lies on her side and supports her head on the hand of one bent arm, the other arm stretches along the length of her body, the elbow fits into the slight dip where her waist comes. Rupa feels her sister's attention surround her, envelope her, depriving her of air. Jayanti's physical closeness and intrusive stare cause a reaction in Rupa who wants to move away, to regain her distance, but can't for fear of offence.

"Well, how is she? Tell me, tell me all about her. I want to hear everything. Have you brought photographs?" The shock of hearing Ma referred to directly confuses Rupa. Previously Jayanti colluded with the family rules of evasion, of denial, behaving as if Rupa came from nowhere, as if she was not connected personally, humanly, with her family. Rupa wonders what has prompted her to break the rules now. Jayanti rests a hand on her younger sister's entwined fingers and squeezes them, and this time with a note of pleading, "Did she send any message, any letter for me?" This is different, Sunil and Chhaya make her feel welcome, Priya and Bijoy adore her, but Jayanti is demanding something.

Rupa has to sit up. Moving up the bed so that her back rests against the carved headboard and pulling her skirt down round her ankles, gives her time to recover. The strange thing is Ma isn't up here in Jayanti's room, in the only place where her existence has been acknowledged.

"She's okay, in good health I mean. A bit overweight perhaps, but the doctor isn't worried about that. She's careful about what she eats and she walks everywhere just for the exercise. She's happy enough, always busy." Jayanti holds her gaze steadily – this isn't what she really wants to hear and she's waiting for more.

She wants to know if Ma ever wonders, as she does, how it might have been if she hadn't left.

"What else can I tell you? She's doing the same job, with the Care Agency. Working mostly with older people. They all like it when she's looking after them, she's very popular, they say she's very gentle. Takes her time and doesn't rush them. The pay's not particularly good but she likes the job. She'll be able to retire next year but she hasn't decided yet whether she will or not."

Jayanti looks down at the bed cover which is made from torn strips of sari spun into long strings and woven together with sewing thread. She plucks at the strands, coaxing them back into neat parallel lines with her thumb nail, much as a tennis player rearranges the racket strings after a rally.

"Listen, Jayanti didi, no she doesn't ever speak of you or of Sunil dada or ask about the children or anyone here. She never talks of anything that happened before she arrived, we arrived, in England, and because she never refers to it, I don't ask. I can't ask. Can you imagine, for twenty-eight years she's not spoken about it, about what went wrong? If sometimes she wonders about her own relatives, and she surely must do, she doesn't tell me, or if she remembers how it felt to go away leaving you and Sunil dada behind ... nothing. She knows I write to you all and she sees your letters arrive for me, but she never asks. So how could she send you a message, and how can I tell you how she feels?"

Jayanti climbs wearily off the bed and picks up her sari, signalling to Rupa with her eyes that she should help fold it. When they've finished she takes the folded sari and hangs it over the alna, smoothing it out with her flat palm, and tidies the other clothes already hanging there, refolding and replacing them. Rupa can't see her sister's face, but knows she has to continue speaking for a while. She decides that this is her opportunity to ask what she's come to ask, after all Jayanti herself began the conversation.

"That's one of the things I want to do while I'm here this time, find out more about when they were first married and when you and Sunil dada were young. I've been putting together "Life Story Books" for some of the children on my caseload and...."

"What story books?" Jayanti turns round frowning.

"For the children who've been in Care since they were young, to provide them with a record of their lives. Sometimes they've stayed with so many different foster families and changed social worker so often, no one can remember where they originally came from, how they arrived in Care in the first place. They need to have all the details of their own families even if they're pretty depressing sometimes, usually in fact. So it occurred to me I should do the same for myself, not my life exactly because I know about that, but my background." They are both sitting on the bed now, legs crossed, knees lightly touching. Jayanti's mood has altered, she's happy to be useful, a source of knowledge.

"I'll tell you what I can, any details which would help. You know it was Miss Featherstone who actually arranged their marriage? She came to see you in England a few times, didn't she. And you know Ma was from a Hindu family, and was baptised so she could marry Baba?" Rupa didn't know. Obviously the marriage had been arranged, but by a missionary, and only after Ma had converted? She remembers Miss Featherstone, a tall jolly lady with a sallow complexion who gave her children's books and sensible shoes and put an arm round Ma. Why did Ma's family go along with the suggestion, had she herself wanted to become Christian? The idea that Ma was once Hindu is amazing, for her life is centered even more on the Church than on her work, to which she is devoted. Jayanti is still talking, this is her professional role, to impart information and check it has been understood.

"I know where Ma's family lived because she often took Sunil dada and me there to meet them. A big house, part of it was a goldsmith's shop. I suppose her brothers still live there but we very rarely heard from them – not any more. Only once or twice they tried to send presents for Priya and Bijoy, but Sunil dada wouldn't keep them in case it upset Baba. As for finding out why she left, at first Sunil dada and I used to make up all sorts of reasons and talk about it whenever we were alone. I was only six when it happened, the same age as Bijoy is now, so I can't remember the details, just lots of memories. Impressions and feelings really, no clear details. Sunil dada was ten, so he'd have understood better. Gradually we stopped talking

31

about it as we got older, and Baba never explained anything. I suppose he was too upset."

"What have you told people round here about her? Some of the older people in Church, those who knew Baba's family, must have heard rumors surely?"

"When we first came here Baba told everyone his wife had a serious illness that could only be treated abroad and that was why she had to live there. I think most people suspect she's mad." Rupa is shocked by the matter of fact way in which Jayanti says this.

She wakes up in the night, disorientated and sweating, then notices the fine mesh in which she is enclosed, and remembers. She lies awake watching the circling fireflies, and wondering what sex would be like under a mosquito net with an audience of fireflies.

The night belongs to the dogs; all day they cringe and slink to avoid attention, but at night they perform musical dramas involving a cast drawn from a wide area. Background sounds are supplied by the endless fax machine sizzle and song of crickets, intermittent cycle bells and thud of running feet, dull clink of kitchen pots and bouts of muffled conversation, but the main dialogue and chorus is canine. One dog opens with a bark to which another responds by howling, followed swiftly by other barks and howls in different keys and with different rhythms, the volume depending on whether they come from nearby or from a distance. Then all fall silent and only the background noises remain until it's the turn of another protagonist to begin the next sequence. If only there was a dog god to do for dogs what Ganesh has done for elephants or Hanuman for monkeys, or if they had been attributed the sacred status enjoyed by cows (in theory at least). Not all dogs are like this though, from the taxi Rupa had seen guard dogs on roofs, and Bijoy says one of his friends keeps a dog as a pet.

Sounds and sensations from the external world fade, as her body dissolves again into sleep only thought remains. Rupa wonders how it came to pass, who was involved in planning and securing the marriage, whether it was done willingly or with coercion. But she can't hold onto the thoughts as they separate and snake away in various directions

Mary Featherstone was on her knees in front of the trunk which served as a bench for her visitors, mostly for children in fact because she wasn't sure it would stand an adult's weight. She removed the fitted cover which had been specially made by a local tailor and lifted the lid, letting it fall back against the wall for the stays had long since broken. The trunk was lined with lead to make it insect-proof and the wooden body was strengthened with broad metal strips riveted along all its edges. The whole was painted black and her uncle's name was written in an elegant hand in white paint on the side, along with a variety of official stamps declaring that the trunk was "Shipped by King, King & Co., Bombay" and that it was "Baggage Not Wanted On Voyage." The trunk that accompanied Captain Thomas Featherstone when he served in the Punjab Light Horse Infantry at the beginning of the century, was being used over fifty years later by his niece who served the cause of the Gospel in this land.

Mary derived great pleasure from taking out warm clothes for the winter months. All year she couldn't bear to touch wool, just the thought of it sickened her and made her skin itch, but now in the month of November, in anticipation of the evening and early morning chill, she could happily sort through the trunk's contents. Even the smell of naphthalene which scratched the back of her throat as soon as she opened the lid, could not diminish her enjoyment. She picked up an olive green Kashmiri shawl, a gift from a local businessman around the time he sought admission to the Mission School for his only son. The color didn't suit her yellowish complexion, which she attributed to years of swallowing malaria pills, but it was a warm shawl and embroidered in fine needlework. A couple more shawls for everyday wear, an assortment of cardigans presented to her by the link parishes back home when she visited on deputation during furloughs, one misshapen garment she had knitted herself, and numerous pairs of socks. As she bent forward to reach the blankets stored neatly at the bottom of the trunk, with the intention of spreading them out to check whether the fabric had worn thin along the lines of the folds, there was a light knock on the open door. She turned her head to see a figure standing in the doorway, a tall broad-shouldered man with too much hair, cut very short in order to render it manageable.

"Come in Mr. Koshy, I'm not praying, just sorting through warm clothes for the winter!" She stood up laughing and smoothed her dress down over her knees. George Koshy's top lip trembled awkwardly rather in the manner of a camel, but there was no smile, just an embarrassed snort. Mary's pale blue eyes sparkled, she was determined not to have her mood spoilt by his earnest demeanor. *Come on, George, smile for once, you won't be damned for sharing a joke with me.*

"I can see you are busy, Miss Featherstone, so I won't keep you long, but I wanted to speak with you about your driver. He's your personal driver not a school employee so it's your responsibility to discipline him, all the same you must realize that his actions affect the reputation of the whole school. This is a Christian school and therefore Christian staff, whether they are teachers or drivers, are the examples by which the guardians and everyone else in the township judge Christianity itself." The delivery sounded like a prepared speech which would be quite in keeping with Mr. Koshy's style. For him nothing just happened, everything was carefully planned, whereas Mary was impulsive and could turn on a sixpence.

"What about my driver? What's he done this time? Talking to the children after class, picking flowers from the school garden again?" The cheerful smile remained as she turned to close the lid of the trunk and replace its cover.

"I'm afraid it's more serious than that. I've received a report that he joined in the Kali bhashan procession to the river last night, and that his behavior indicated he was under the influence of alcohol or drugs." George Koshy's head was slightly bowed, and he held his hands together in front of him in a stance which communicated apologetic sympathy. Mary sat down weakly on the trunk and put her hands to her face, shaking her head repeatedly in dismay. Muttering that he'd leave her to think about it, and nodding in a concerned way but clearly anxious to avoid witnessing any display of emotion, Mr. Koshy backed clumsily out of the room banging an elbow on the doorframe as he did so. Mary stayed where she was for a while, then with a sigh walked over to her own chair where she sat rocking miserably back and forth.

Dear Lord ... why? Why was no one grateful for the efforts she made on their behalf, why did they all repay her with disobedience, irresponsibility, dishonesty, rudeness ... ? Not only her driver, although that was serious enough, but the teachers too. The new teacher from Patna, class teacher of II B, disappeared one evening upon receiving a telegram which, according to her roommate, read simply – "Come at once." There had been no communication from her since. Mary guessed this meant either a marriage proposal or the offer of a better job, but why not let the school know what was happening? After all the girl's own mother was a headmistress and her father a doctor, surely they should behave like decent Christians.

The trouble with these people was that they had no sense of responsibility towards anyone except members of their own family. When would they realize they were part of a Christian family too, and had duties to the Church and to the Mission School? Then someone on the staff organized a petition demanding higher wages for qualified teachers, claiming they were paid well below government salary scales. But didn't they realize the school supported itself solely out of the fees charged, didn't they appreciate the fact that at least they had a job? And then of course there was always trouble in the Teachers' Mess; accusations of money being paid in but not recorded, people surreptitiously taking food back to their rooms for those who hadn't contributed, endless complaints about the amount of chilli and salt used, and the cooking methods. Even the former hostel superintendent from Madras found the Mess impossible to manage, so he'd handed her back the records of expenditure, and now who was going to run it?

Then Mary's thoughts returned to her driver. His elderly father took care of her when she first arrived in Bengal, the most attentive servant she had ever known. A man who took pity on the township dogs and, crouching beside them, pulled lice from their raw and mangy backs. Who rescued moths from their love affair with electric light bulbs and, softly tutting, carried them in cupped hands to be released back into the night. Whose skilful hands massaged Mary's feet and legs when she had high fever, until in her delirium she cried out for him to stop. Last year the old man brought his son from the village and begged her to find some kind of employment for the boy, touched her feet and wept. For the father's sake she arranged for the boy to join a basic driving course, and when he passed the test, kept him on as her personal driver, although she really had no need of one. She even supplied a gray uniform with peaked cap! He was quick-tempered and unpredictable and, she suspected, not altogether safe behind the wheel, but she continued to employ him because of her promise to his father.

And now George came and gloated, no that wasn't fair, he was as upset by the reports as she was, but he had been quick to stress the fact that her driver was personally employed by her and not the school. Well, she would summon her driver this evening. He would be embarrassed if she went to his quarters in E colony, the very basic accommodation provided for unskilled manual workers. (Only the General Manager lived in an A type dwelling, B colony was occupied by senior managers and the other township employees were spread between C and D according to rank.) Mary had been to her driver's quarters once when he was ill, really ill with typhoid, but his wife wouldn't allow her inside because she was ashamed of their living conditions. This evening she would tell him that if his behavior didn't improve he'd have to return to his village.

36

Mary picked up her Bible, read a portion and then closed her eyes in prayer. As she prayed her muscles relaxed, her mouth formed into a quiet smile, and her breathing slowed. By the time she left her room to go along to chapel for evening prayers, her shoulders were pulled back, her chin lifted and her eyes had regained their sparkle.

Staff attendance at evening prayers was another cause for sorrow, but although only George Koshy and three others came today, she would not let that dishearten her. It was her turn to lead the worship, and she chose the Bible passage she had just read in her room, Jeremiah chapter 13 verses 1 to 11, where God tells the Prophet to buy a loincloth, wear it for a while, and then hide it in a crevice in the rocks. When, at God's command, Jeremiah returned to retrieve the loincloth, it was spoilt and useless. Mary told them the cloth represented the Israelites, or in their case the Church. If they stayed close to God just as a loincloth clings to the waist, then they would become God's own people, but if they didn't, like the discarded loincloth they too would be useless. She wanted to share with them the comfort which she gained from this passage, she said. It taught her that God could use even the most ordinary objects and events to show people that they must change. Objects and events which, when seen through a prophet's eyes, carried a message powerful beyond mere words.

As Mary walked back to her room she passed a group of dogs fighting, their screams and ferocious snarls more vicious than usual. There was an established pack which claimed the township as its territory, and usually an outsider straying inside the boundary would be chased off pretty quickly. But this time it seemed the intruder was putting the others to flight, which suggested it might be a mad dog. She must remember to inform Security so they could observe the stranger, and then they would probably shoot it.

When Mary reached her room a short figure was standing in the darkness outside. Cheerfully she opened the door and her driver followed her inside, but instead of crouching on the floor as was his habit, he moved restlessly from foot to foot as if limbering up for two rounds in the ring. His eyes were bloodshot, his hair dry and uncombed, and his expression told her he guessed what

37

was coming. Making an effort to keep her voice light but serious, she told him what she had heard and asked him if it was true. Instead of vehemently denying it as she'd anticipated, he exploded into loud complaints about how poorly paid he was, how terrible his quarters were and how he was only allowed to drive her little toy car and not a real car, an Ambassador for instance.

"But I have no Ambassador!" she exclaimed, and he replied defiantly, "If you were a *real memsahib* you'd buy one."

Resisting the urge to laugh aloud, Mary warned him to remember what he was taught by the Christians in his village, by his Sunday School teachers and by his Padre babu, and she chided him for his drinking and for mixing with the Kali worshippers. He became subdued, crouching down in his usual way and nodding sullenly. She threatened to send him back to his father if his behavior didn't improve. His muttered protests continued for a while until finally she prayed with him, asking forgiveness from God and pronouncing her own.

Mary awoke in the night to find the idea had been growing in her head even while she slept. Slowly it was becoming more definite, less an idea more a plan. Exactly what she would do she wasn't sure, but she hoped it would be something really significant, something akin to a prophetic symbol though not as dramatic of course. She would discuss it with James Lawson who was due to arrive tomorrow for his annual visit, for the purpose of supplying her with spiritual guidance and support.

For lunch next day Mary served up a cheese flan she'd made using a tin of cheese bought in New Market during her last trip to Calcutta. She went to Calcutta twice a year to have her hair cut and permed at *Fanny Moonlight's*, a Chinese hairdresser's, and always took the opportunity while she was there to buy delicacies from New Market. The small print on the tin said it should be kept refrigerated, but by the time she got it home the metal was uncomfortably hot to touch. Now, however, as part of the flan, it was thoroughly cooked. James Lawson had been in India longer than her, surely his stomach would have no difficulty digesting a slightly dubious cheese flan.

"How are things at school then, Mary? Is George Koshy shaping up as well as you hoped?" James rested his elbows on the checked tablecloth, removed the white crocheted cover edged with colored beads from his glass, and sipped the boiled water. His voice was mellow and his eyes kind, just the right person for the post. The job was tiring though, involving extensive travel. Last week Bihar, next week Orissa, and then back to base in Bombay for a fortnight to catch up on his correspondence.

"George, I mean Mr. Koshy – I've tried hard to get on first name terms but he just won't call me Mary – is a fine upstanding Christian. An honest and hard-working man who's committed to building this school up and to making it successful." Mary came over to the table carrying a plate in each hand and gestured to James to remove his elbows, rather as if he was a naughty boy. He caught her eye and chuckled as he complied.

"But?"

"Well, I sometimes think the Almighty was low on supplies of humor when he created our Mr. Koshy. He's so terribly earnest, never relaxes or opens up. In fact he's uncomfortable with emotions of any kind." They bowed their heads while James said a simple grace, then helped themselves to boiled vegetables seasoned only with salt and black pepper, and began eating. She knew he remained silent to give her time to unburden herself spiritually. His role was to act as confidante and advisor on matters spiritual, but she didn't divide easily into the conventional divisions of body, mind and spirit. With her, everything got mixed up and activity ruled the lot. So she decided to broach the subject of her idea, as that was both spirit and action.

"There's little commitment generally amongst staff, internal squabbles, disobeying school rules, missing prayers, you know what it's like. No energy, no passion for the Lord and His work. I've been feeling for a while they needed something to shock them out of their lethargy, and after hearing about my driver yesterday...."

"What about your driver?" She told him what she'd heard, and was annoyed when James looked amused. "Go on," he said, serious once more.

"After Mr. Koshy left my room I happened to open my Bible at Jeremiah 13...."

"The loincloth?"

"That's right. The whole concept of a prophetic sign, symbolic act or whatever you want to call it, really appeals to me. I've run out of words and they're deaf to my words in any case, but if I could do something to grab their attention and stir them up." She paused, "Don't look so alarmed, James, I'm not about to rip off my dress and go and hide it in the branches of a mango tree!" It was her turn to be amused. They had finished the flan so she removed the plates and cutlery, and began organizing the pancakes which she would serve with molasses and pieces of lime for squeezing. He sat there deep in thought, not offering to help, and she contemplated chiding him about his idleness but decided to let it go.

"In theory it sounds a possibility, it all depends on what you choose to do. I'd recommend much prayer and patient waiting on the Lord before you do anything. What about discussing the idea with your Deputy first? I think you told me the Bishop wanted George Koshy to take over all responsibility from you next year, so perhaps he should be involved from the outset." She hadn't thought of sharing her idea with George, he would dissect and analyze it so thoroughly there'd be no joy left in it.

The following day James led a Quiet Day for the teaching staff. Attendance was almost one hundred percent, the atmosphere in the chapel reverent and calm. He was skilful in this role, combining readings, meditation, address and discussion in just the right proportions so that no one became bored. She was impressed by the sincerity of the comments and questions from her staff when they reflected together on the Bible passages. How well they responded to the presence of an outsider! He was made to feel welcome during the refreshment breaks too, people outdid each other in their efforts to take care of him, to see he had all he needed. If only it would last. The same changes occurred whenever new staff arrived, but as the weeks went by everyone slipped back into their old habits of bickering and selfish apathy.

But what if someone joined them who didn't know about being a Christian, someone who would need guidance and care over a prolonged period? While preparing for teaching practice when she was at college, Mary had realized you only fully understood something when you had to teach it, to explain it to another person. How could she engineer the arrival of such an outsider? It must happen in the natural course of events, nothing out of the ordinary, that was the point. Only experienced Christians were eligible for teaching appointments, so a new member of staff wouldn't fit the bill. And then it came to her, and she pressed fingernails into the palms of clenched fists and disguised the shout by pretending to cough.

Mary's driver sulked as he drove to the station, taking James to catch a train onwards to his next destination. Mary sat in the passenger seat, reprimanding him whenever he swerved sharply, bumped over a particularly rough piece of road instead of avoiding it or stalled the engine which happened quite frequently. His driving deteriorated in direct proportion to her criticisms. From his uncomfortable situation in the back seat James interrupted her, suggesting she refrain from comment until the return journey as he wanted to reach the station in one piece. She laughed aloud and directed her attention towards James instead. Her driver, not understanding English, thought James was adding his own criticism. To serve them right he took his left hand off the wheel and laid it idly on his uniformed thigh. His right elbow rested on the top edge of the open window while he steered with fingertips only lightly touching the wheel, hoping to provoke them further.

"It's been lovely to have you with us, I rarely get to talk *English* English with anyone. You know what I mean, Indian English can be so shallow. I never learnt Bengali well enough to have deep conversations in that language, just what I call 'kitchen Bangla,' enough to talk to servants and wives and little children. I didn't take to language school in Darjeeling somehow. I managed the 'What is this? This is a pen; What is that? That is a chair,' stage alright, but once we got into more complex sentences I was floundering. I can understand most things, but when it comes to speaking...." There was a pause during which she tried not to notice her driver's antics.

"James, I can't thank you enough for yesterday, it really was spiritually enriching, for everyone I think. I was surprised at how people opened up and spoke of their own spiritual condition. You should come more often."

"Surely you could find someone to come out from Calcutta, say once a month, once a term at least? I can't do more than my annual stint I'm afraid. But I agree, I felt your staff were really committed to the discipline and demands of the Quiet Day. Very rewarding for me too." James smiled as he recollected the warmth of their fellowship.

Twisting further round towards James, trying to keep the excitement out of her voice, "Going back to what I was saying the evening you arrived, I wondered about bringing in an outsider, someone who doesn't know much about Christianity. The staff would renew their own faith as they taught the newcomer, adopt the role of experts instead of being treated always like children. Then I remembered the prophet Hosea, even his choice of a wife was prophetic. 'Go, take to yourself a wife of harlotry, and have children of harlotry, for the land commits great harlotry by forsaking the Lord.' Startled by the dramatic tone in which Mary delivered this quotation, her driver clutched at the wheel with both hands and stalled the engine.

"No, no start second gear! I tell you start first gear." And then to James again, "A sign to end all signs! Perhaps I could find a Hindu bride for one of our staff? I know it's usually frowned upon, but this would be for a very special purpose. It just might be possible to find a Hindu girl whose parents were prepared for her to become Christian, in order to obtain a good son-in-law, especially one with a secure job." Mary continued, pleading with James to share her enthusiasm.

They overtook a lumbering bullock cart in the face of a bus which lurched one-sidedly towards them, just returning to their side of the road to hear the bus's horn reach full volume as it passed them, close enough for their car to be shaken by the draught.

Mary couldn't tell whether James' expression was a reaction to her words or to the alarming proximity of the bus.

"Come on, Mary, that would be rather extreme wouldn't you say? You can't just lift something that happened in Palestine two thousand years ago and apply it in India today, you know that! Sounds like dangerous manipulation to me. I really would counsel caution." A trace of impatience at the edge of his voice warned her that she had told him too much, that she must hatch this plan herself and bring it to pass in her own time, or rather in God's time for the whole idea had for her the aura of divine prompting.

They reached the station and her driver revved the engine fiercely before switching it off. He dragged the large canvas bag out of the boot and dropped it at James' feet, then went off to sit on a low bench at the tea stall where he lit a biri from the smoldering rope hanging there. James raised his eyebrows in faint disapproval of this casual behavior, and Mary shook her head in exasperation, mumbling that she couldn't do much about him on account of his father who was a dear friend. Her failure to discipline her driver reminded her of the way Indian parents indulged their offspring, they loved them too much to be consistently strict. They left him boasting to anyone who would listen, of the adventurous journeys he'd undertaken with the memsahib, while he drank milky-sweet spiced tea from a glass.

James and Mary stood on the platform where a number of fellow travelers and station dwellers drifted together to stand and stare, some self-consciously, turning away when Mary smiled in their direction, others open-mouthed and unabashed, completely absorbed by the spectacle. She bought guavas from the baskets set out at the back of the platform, searching for the few pale ripe ones amidst the heap of hard dark green fruit they liked to chew, preferably with a little salt, and then spit out – disgusting habit! She would stew the fruit with a little sugar until it turned a delicate pink and then eat it for dessert. Absentmindedly she examined the paper bag made from the page of a used exercise book, in which the fruit had been handed to her, checking it hadn't come from her school. Once she saw a correction on a bag which horrified her; "the boy has a book" was crossed out, presumably by a teacher, and replaced by "the boy have a book." Fortunately, the exercise book from which that bag came was unlike those used in the Mission School.

When it was announced that his train had been delayed, James insisted she wait no longer as it would be unsafe to travel after dusk. It was tacitly agreed between them her driver would be little use in the event of attack by dacoits. Too excitable. No more was said about her plan, but as he kissed her cheek and pressed her hand firmly in farewell, he looked into her soul and his eyes warned her to be sensible.

There was one particular teacher, Nirmal Sarkar, whom Mary had in mind as a potential groom. He was a sensible young man, conscientious about his work, able to mix well with other staff, and a sincere believer. A bit emotional perhaps, like all Bengalis. He wept once during Assembly when she made an announcement concerning a child in his class who had died suddenly of gastroenteritis. Parents' fault, they refused to take him to hospital because it was an inauspicious Thursday, and by Friday he was so weak and dehydrated the hospital couldn't help. The child was one of Nirmal's favorites, it was school policy to treat all pupils equally of course but no one could help having favorites, just as long as it didn't show. Yes, Nirmal would be perfect. His widowed mother died last year and his younger sister had recently been married off to an engineer. She now lived with her in-laws in the family home in Bombay, so Nirmal had no immediate family either to object to her proposal or for whom he was responsible.

Mary sipped her early morning glass of hot water, the best way she'd found of keeping her bowels regular. How to proceed from here? She would pray of course, every step of the way, and call Nirmal and put the idea to him in vague outline. It would help if she explained her reasons, then he'd feel he was involved in important work for the Lord. She had some thoughts about a bride too, better not to mention them just yet. Keep it general and test his reaction. She stood up quickly and hurried into her bathroom. The glass of hot water rarely failed her.

CHAPTER FOUR
1999

Rupa stands in front of her room, getting ready to go out. She's placed her cup and saucer on the top edge of a metal grill and balanced the mirror on top of a cement pillar. From this level you are closed in, trunks and branches rather than leaves take the eye, the scenery is more intimate than the broad view from the roof but still beautiful, especially in the morning light. Two hens peck around the channel leading from the pump, hoping to find stray grains of rice washed off the evening plates. A dog with curly tail squeezes through a gap in the fence and noses despondently at the edge of a shallow pit half-filled with rubbish. At the far end of the garden Rupa can see Sunil occupied with his pigeons.

"My dad's going to come back as a pigeon" Bijoy had informed Rupa earlier, adding without hesitation, "and I'll be a mango tree". Chhaya joined in the game, "I suppose I'll be a cooking pot, I seem to spend most of my time in the kitchen." "And I'll be a daaaaance!" contributed Priya with a flourish of her hands. The children looked expectantly at Rupa. Nothing came to mind, what would she be? "I'll be a princess who never grows up," she said.

The last few days have been spent eating, bathing, washing clothes, lying on the bed squashed between Bijoy and Priya to rest after food; slicing onions and bitter gourd, cutting potatoes, beguns, bhindis and serving tea to curious neighbors who had come to meet the visitor from abroad; helping Bijoy to commit his English lessons to memory and entertaining Priya's girlfriends ("Tell us, Pishi, who do you think was a better person, Princess Diana or Mother Teresa?"). Rupa has floated wherever the family has taken her, the relief of loosing her own weight is wonderful. No decisions more significant than whether to accept another piece of fish, to walk to the sweet shop or go by ricksha, and when she gets there whether to buy shondesh or pantua. But today's program is more adventurous, Jayanti and Rupa will accompany Priya to a dance workshop organized by a local dancing master and led by a famous television personality. Nirmal Babu's objections to the outing have rumbled on for days but so far Chhaya has kept the situation from erupting.

"It says in the Bible that King David danced before the Lord!" Priya's wail detaches itself from the general morning noises.

"Stupid! That was another kind of dance. Hindus dance but Christians don't. Aren't you ashamed to show yourself off like that now that you're growing into a woman? Your father's a fool not to stop you." The pitch of Nirmal babu's voice is rising and Rupa suspects more than religious prejudice is at stake here, but there's no need to worry on Priya's account, she's more than a match for her grandfather. Rupa wants to know how this will develop so tidies away her mirror, comb and makeup, and goes downstairs to finish drinking her tea on the veranda.

Priya is standing in front of the mirror, practising dancing postures. Chhaya looks up from rearranging the bedding, opens her eyes wide and shakes her head in warning, her lips forming the words, "Be quiet!" Priya pouts and flounces off to the kitchen where Jayanti is packing a tiffin box and water bottle into her bag.

"Listen, Jayanti pishi, listen to what Dadu's saying! Can you make him understand? Tell him dancing is a cultural thing, an Indian thing, and it's alright for Christians to do it." Priya has learnt to maneuver within the tight limits of her family and is becoming an expert in small scale diplomacy. Jayanti leaves her preparations, rinses then shakes her hands, rubs them on the crumpled pleats of her sari and walks purposefully into Nirmal babu's room.

"Look, Baba, listen to me. Priya's school results aren't very good – are they? Supposing, when the time comes, she doesn't do well in her final exams, what chance has she of getting a job?" Jayanti aims to be firm but reasonable. "At least if she gets some dancing certificates she can earn money giving dance lessons. Times have changed, and nowadays girls have to be self-sufficient. Don't you know that?" They both know he's heard this argument a hundred times before and that Jayanti will take Priya to the workshop today in spite of his protests. He doesn't have the energy to argue it out with this daughter of his, so picks up his Bible and continues to mumble objections as he turns the pages, the principal function of which seems to be as a storage place for the numerous bits of folded paper placed between them.

"There are two children in my school whose parents wanted to withdraw them from any lessons which mention the Mahabharat or Ramayan. Can you imagine anything so stupid! I called the parents to school and explained an attitude like that would create problems for their children's education. They're wonderful stories, part of our heritage."

Rupa is surprised by the stirring of pity she feels for her father, relieved to find she's not completely heartless. Jayanti doesn't know when she's won, when it's time to stop, she's dangerously close to destroying the outward respect to which Nirmal babu is entitled. He's had enough and escapes, shuffling out in his loose sandals to take up his customary position in the deck chair on the veranda. Bijoy follows him, standing behind the chair he begins to tickle his grandfather's bald head, ignoring the indulgent protests. Nirmal babu suddenly notices Rupa standing by the steps, and realizes that she has witnessed the whole scene. Then he sees his estranged wife standing beside Rupa, resting one hand on her daughter's shoulder, the other held out to plead with him as she sadly shakes her head. She's telling him she agrees with Jayanti, but her objection is less strident. Nirmal babu looks agitated and turns away. Rupa glances behind her and sees at once what's happened.

"No one's going to be there to see Priya dancing, you know Baba, only the other girls and their guardians." Chhaya, sitting on the iron bed, uses a conciliatory tone. "In any case it'll be too crowded to see clearly. To tell the truth, I think dancing's good for her health, she doesn't really get any other exercise."

The hall is enormous and has a very high ceiling from which fans hang down on long metal rods. It reminds Rupa of a minor stately home, built with elegance in mind but now appearing scruffy for lack of attention. Crowning the stage is an elaborate triangle supported by columns and decorated with twirls and scrolls in plaster molding picked out in blue and pink. Just below the stage is a simple arrangement of clay pots containing lighted candles and incense sticks, surrounded by white patterns traced on the floor. An area in front of this is covered with large cloth mats, then there is clear floor space up to the rows of chairs set out towards the back of the hall. Most of these chairs are already occupied, but Jayanti stakes claim to two near the front, firmly pushing aside other people's bags which lie near them on the floor. This embarrasses Rupa but she says nothing, determined to fit in, to behave as if she does this sort of a thing every day. In the house she happily admits her westernness, her ignorance of how things should be done, and the children have great fun teaching her, but in public she is rather tense, anxious not to draw attention to herself. Jayanti is in charge of the party, proud of her niece and aware of the questioning glances directed at her younger sister. Rupa will not let her down.

All the while Priya is looking around with shining eyes and greeting her friends, soon she disappears amongst the throng of chattering, laughing girls. Everywhere mothers and aunties fix clips and slides and colored bands in long hair, oiled and tightly plaited or more loosely bound with locks escaping to hang round ears and the napes of necks, and in short bouncy hair which is more difficult to tame. Long scarves are draped across chests and firmly pinned to shoulders to disguise the line of swelling breasts. Someone asks Jayanti for safety pins and she produces a generous supply which she is happy to distribute to the less well-organized.

Everyone wears the standard salwar kameez, made of every kind of material from lustrous silks to stiff cottons, from business-like plain white to contrasting and co-ordinating color schemes. Sisters wear the same outfits, or the same colors but in reverse combinations. Rupa notices that many of the costumes are green with pink scarves, probably the prescribed colors of a previous function. Girls hang pearls or gold chains round their necks while others look on enviously and whisper together that these aren't proper for the occasion, for a serious dancing class. Strings of bells are wound tightly round ankles on top of trousers so that they don't chaff the skin. Some strings are so short they give barely more than a single row of bells, others have six or more rows stretching halfway up to the knee. Rupa wonders whether the number of rows is significant, reflecting the wearer's status. Feet are stamped experimentally to make sure the knots won't work loose during the class, until the hall is filled with the shaking of rattle snakes.

The atmosphere reminds Rupa of her time at school, those painful prize days, sports days, school plays and pantomimes. As a child she only wanted not to be noticed, desperately hoping her mother would wear or do or say nothing to make her the butt of jokes in next day's playground. When she was older, at Parents' Evenings Rupa was humiliated by her mother's less than perfect English as she sat at little tables opposite the subject teachers and discussed her daughter's progress. But equally she was angry with her teachers for addressing Ma in voices loud and slow, as if she was deaf or lacked intelligence. When teachers directed their replies at Rupa, she would lower her eyes, refusing to interpret so that they were forced to communicate with Ma directly.

Someone on the stage is testing the sound system, blowing across the microphone and muttering into it. He begins to address the hall in sonorous dramatic style, welcoming the famous dance instructor and television presenter who is to conduct today's workshop. As he speaks, various dignitaries walk onto the stage, guided by the local dancing master, and sit along the back behind a table on which a picture of Rabindranath Tagore, the revered poet and composer of songs, is displayed. A few of the girls and their guardians notice the procession and nudge and frown at each other to keep quiet, but most continue to bustle and fidget.

Priya has returned and Jayanti is busy with the finishing touches. Rupa listens silently to the speaker's words, the language of this formal address demands her concentration. The dancers are called to sit on the mats beneath the stage, a frenzy of last minute adjustments leaks away into a stream flowing towards the front where it subsides into a still pool. The dancing master takes the microphone, his calm slow tones contrasting with those of the previous announcer. Guardians fall silent as he thanks everyone for coming, supervises the offering of garlands to those on the stage, and finally hands over to the guest instructor to begin.

She is wrapped in an insipid yellow sari, the color of dried river mud. There are folds of fat round her neck and fat bulges out in the gap between the end of her blouse and her waistline. Her upper arms are heavy and her neck has disappeared into the curve of her shoulders. Even the features of her face have no beauty, her eyes are dull behind over-sized frames, and her thinning hair has been strained into a small knot. She says she is pleased to be there but when she speaks her voice has no warmth, no magic.

The seated audience becomes restless as a shuffle of doubt passes through it. Jayanti whispers loudly that she's not wasting a whole day if the instructor proves to be incompetent. The dancers are preoccupied with themselves and notice nothing. The woman on the stage tells them to stand, but there is not enough dancing space so the rows of chairs have to be moved back a few more feet, which is done with maximum fuss and expressions of annoyance.

Te te, ta ta, thoi thoi ...

A clear rhythmic voice chants from the group of musicians at the edge of the hall. On the stage the instructor rotates her shoulders, gracefully stretches out one arm, turns her palm upwards her eyes following the line of her supple fingers, and strikes two firm beats with her heel. The children are all watching her, no

50

one in the audience moves. She performs the step again, adding a perfectly controlled flick of the wrist and head, and commands them to copy, her voice powerful and assured. The tabla gives the rhythm, then they hear the first line of the song.

Who is this   forever dancing   in my soul?
Who is playing   endless rhythms   for the dancer?

The tune climbs slowly up from the depths, two steps up and one down, then falls away again. She pinches a fold of sari between thumb and forefinger of both hands, lifting it just enough to reveal delicate ankles which move with such speed and lightness that they can't follow.

Ta ta thoi thoi   ta ta thoi thoi   ta ta thoi thoi.

Lord Shiva dances over the world's surface. She leaps, twists, stamps back and forth over the stage, introducing more complex rhythms, more elaborate steps. Demanding their total attention, she scolds them, encourages them, praises them. The audience can see her through a forest of moving arms, hear her through the thud of many feet and the jingle of a hundred bells.

Dance of birth   dance of death   side by side.
Freedom dancing   slavery dancing   day and night.
Ta ta thoi thoi   ta ta thoi thoi   ta ta thoi thoi.

Lord Shiva circles the world – Nataraj – to a mesmerizing and relentless rhythm.

"I can remember Ma putting jasmine flowers in her hair and dancing for me, and then dressing me up in a cream sari with a red border and showing me how to do some steps. She laughed because my fingers were so plump I couldn't do the hand positions properly. I recall the feeling of it being our secret, I think she closed the window shutters first and only danced when no one else was at home." Jayanti speaks in a low voice, her tone softer than usual.

51

"Sometimes I've seen her move in tune to her tapes as if she's dancing, really dancing I mean, as if she's learnt properly like this. Once I asked whether she could dance when she was young and she said 'a little,' but nothing more. Baba wouldn't have let her after marriage, would he? I mean, the way he was about letting Priya come today, he'd never have let his wife do it." Rupa replies thoughtfully.

"That's my point. Perhaps it was just one more way in which he stopped her being herself. Perhaps that's also why he's so adverse to Priya dancing – he's frightened she'll turn out like her grandmother."

"What do you mean? How did her grandmother turn out?" Rupa is defensive.

"In England. Not part of the family. Away from the Christian fold, as far as Baba is concerned. I'm not on his side, just trying to understand how he feels and why she left. She could have found the restrictions impossible to accept." Jayanti's response is immediate.

"It's not enough. She would have minded that of course, but it's not enough to make her leave. If she did leave, that is. You don't know her like I do. You think she would stand up for herself and believe in women having rights over their own lives. But she isn't really like that. It's the way you think, so you think she must have too." Rupa intends only to examine and analyze Jayanti's suggestion not to undermine her, but from the way she hunches her shoulders it is clear her sister is annoyed. Rupa wishes she'd been more sensitive. Of course there must be a reason why Jayanti created this picture of Ma, a strong-minded and independent woman, perhaps to avoid admitting her own feelings about being abandoned. You have to find a way to understand your mother's desertion.

She tries to defuse the moment. "What about singing? Wouldn't he object to that too? Ma sings all the time, not only Bengali tunes, English songs as well."

"Why should singing be a problem? Many Christians learn to sing, Baba himself had a lovely voice when he was younger. We always performed kirtan in Church at Christmas and Easter, and there are even some of Rabindranath's songs in our hymnbook." Rupa's tactic has succeeded, the balance is redressed and Jayanti is again the teacher.

The dancing has stopped for a few moments while a fan is maneuvered up onto the stage for the instructor's benefit. Then a young man passes up her handbag from which she takes a handkerchief to wipe her mouth and cheeks, and, having removed her glasses, her eyes and forehead too. She replaces the handkerchief, and hands her bag back to the young man without looking at him.

"Dance is the body's song," she declares, and then signals to the tabla player before demonstrating another sequence. The moment's pause has been enough to distract the younger girls, one or two of whom seek out their mothers' chairs and gulp down a few mouthfuls of water. A hemorrhage of dancers ensues each searching for her own water-bottle holding guardian, snatching at the chance for excited chatter with other dancers. Rupa notices one small girl move from her place in the front towards the back where the older girls are, wind her arms tightly round her sister's neck pulling her off balance so that she stumbles, and kiss her cheek. This could have been Jayanti and her, sisters separated by about the same difference in age.

Perhaps it would have been easier if she'd had a sister to walk to school with, to sit beside at dinnertimes. But she would have hated sharing Ma with someone else.

When Rupa called on her Asian friends their houses swarmed with brothers, sisters, cousins (babies passed from lap to lap, ball games on the grass out at the back), and they found the emptiness of her home strange when she returned the invitation. When Rupa and Ma went anywhere it was just the two of them, except for the day trips by coach with ladies from Church. She wasn't lonely though – having each other was enough.

Now the instructor is dancing with knees bent and pointing outward, impossible to stay like this but she goes through step after step in this position. The audience rustles anxiously, commenting sympathetically to each other on those in the back rows who can't hold this stance, wondering if their child will fall short and be picked out, humiliated in front of the whole hall. The rhythm too is impossible. Rupa leans to one side, craning her neck to catch sight of Priya, to see whether she is managing to keep up.

Ek dui, ek dui ek dui tin. Ek dui, ek dui ek dui tin.

The dancing master goes onto the stage and addresses a few words to the instructor's still dancing face. She nods impatiently and half an hour later reluctantly calls a halt. From the depths of her bag Jayanti produces slices of thinly buttered bread, bananas, shondesh and little salty biscuits. Other children are fed luchis and fried vegetables from stainless steel tiffin boxes. Priya and Jayanti disapprove of this, after so much exertion light refreshment is best they tell each other loudly, and Rupa listens with embarrassment, hoping no one will hear their disparaging comments. Inwardly she smiles at her own reserve, her horror at the thought of causing offence in public. Some mothers didn't get the right information and thought the workshop would end at midday. They sit with grim faces, offering only water and promises of treats when they eventually get home, until their daughters drift off to hang around the edges of groups where there is plenty of food, hoping to be included in the general sharing out. Then the instructor calls them back again.

Because they have rested and taken refreshment the dancers' concentration has improved and they grow in confidence. From behind, guardians see hands and heads move in unison, and hear the shiver and jingle of bells when many feet stamp as one. The audience sighs and their faces melt with pride and pleasure. A young man enters the hall and moves between the rows of chairs, from his clothes Rupa guesses he's probably a driver. One of the women notices him and beckons, pointing out her daughter who is in the middle of the body of dancers, and he strains to get a good view, eventually finding a vantage point standing on a bench at the side of the hall. He is amazed, his face glows with wonder, not at her individual dancing for many times he's watched her practice, but that she is part of this moving whole.

At last the dancers step back, heads bowed, finger tips pressed together in homage to the gods who watch their performance.

In the ricksha coming home they argue about the distribution of prizes. Jayanti complains that it isn't fair to judge someone who's been taking dancing lessons for years against someone who has only just started.

"Of course she won! She's very experienced and helps teach the little ones. No one else had a chance. There should have been separate categories." Priya gets excited and begins to shout, then seeing Rupa's expression, she stops and bursts out laughing at her own anger.

"What do you think, Rupa pishi?"

"What's the point of prizes anyway? You enjoyed yourself didn't you, that's what matters." This isn't the right time for Rupa to explain she thinks prizes are harmful, all they do is introduce competitive divisions.

"What a funny thing to say, you can't invite such a famous person and not ask her to give out prizes!" Fresh laughter bubbles up in Priya. "She'd be very disappointed, wouldn't she Jayanti pishi?"

"Alright then, if there has to be a prize I'd give it you." Rupa wraps her arms more tightly round Priya who is sitting uncomfortably on her knee.

"I know what Bijoy would say, he'd say the person who's the best dancer should get the prize, no matter what. That's how he thinks." Priya says thoughtfully.

They pass the huge skeletons of Kali Puja pandals, great structures of green bamboo bones tied with sinews of rope, a mass of intersecting lines like a draftsman's sketch. Hollow scaffolding which is itself the building. Some already have sections blotted in with colored cloth stretched tight across the frame, so that the draft begins to solidify into a recognizable form. On the ground nearby lie domes and towers already constructed but waiting to be hoisted into position. There is an atmosphere of anticipation as groups of youths congregate proudly in front of their local pandals.

Jayanti insists on stopping at cousin Khuku's house which stands beside the road they travel on. She must have seen Rupa coming and going and will be offended if they don't call in to drink tea. Rupa is happy to comply and Jayanti pays the ricksha fare. Tugging the end of her sari round her neck with one hand while the other holds the pleats free of her feet and the jagged edges of the vehicle frame, Jayanti maneuvers herself out of the seat and down onto the ground with a grunt.

The house is unfinished, jagged holes in the raw brick walls are yet to be filled with window frames and doors. The roof is of thick bamboo poles to which corrugated tin sheets have been secured with wire. Khuku's two youngest children peep shyly round the doorway. The only furniture in the house is one wide bed and a spindly alna, almost invisible beneath its burden of folded clothes. Someone has lined the brick shelves with sheets of newspaper cut at the edge into a feathery fringe, and then arranged stainless steel bowls bottom up in a pyramid for decoration. Priya sits on the bed, legs curled beneath her, head resting on Rupa's shoulder. Rupa can feel the vibrations of her humming.

Ignoring their insistence that they aren't staying long, Khuku sends her son to buy sweets and places a kettle of water on the clay oven. She asks the necessary questions about Rupa's job and marriage prospects but doesn't mention Rupa's mother. She excuses the poor state of her house with tales of strikes and refused loans and her husband's illness. Rupa expresses her sympathy, and is disturbed by the mismatch between Khuku's permanent wide smile and her depressing words. Jayanti appears to find this normal so Rupa concludes it must be a cultural thing.

"Did you go to see the Parishad's protest rally, Jayanti didi? You know, it was in the papers, the West Bengal Christian Council. I went. For one thing I wanted an excuse to go to Calcutta and visit my brother and his family, but I really wanted to join the rally too. There were huge crowds gathered, lots and lots of people, you can't imagine. People from the Roman Catholic side, Buddhists, all sorts were there. We've got to stand up for ourselves. I asked my Hindu neighbors here, 'Will you beat me up and take my house?' and they said, 'No, Boudi, we'll look after you,

56

don't worry.' If anyone attacks me I'll stand up for myself you know, I won't just let them do it."

Khuku raises her fists in the air, her sari drops flat against her chest. The shaping at the front of the blouse which hangs off her sharp shoulders is hollow, but her skin is stretched tight across the bones of her face, eye sockets and jaw line sharply defined. As she waves her arms about, narrow bangles slide loosely up and down. Jayanti enters into the debate with enthusiasm, enjoying Khuku's militant language but arguing another angle. "The Sangh Parivar calls us American and British agents! They tell us to go home! We mustn't let them have any grounds for saying that."

Rupa suspects that the Sangh Parivar, whoever they might be, aren't particularly interested in having grounds for their opinions. The topic under discussion is one of which she knows nothing and she's surprised to see the passion it arouses in the two women. In her experience it's best to keep quiet about one's religious identity. At primary school she was told to describe in her weekend diary how she celebrated Baisakhi or Eid, her teachers always assuming she was either Sikh or Muslim, if indeed they knew the difference. Not Christian at least, she was the wrong color for a Christian, and Rupa hadn't contradicted them. Her Asian friends couldn't understand why she neither went to the temple nor fasted at Ramzan, and if they found out in spite of her attempts to conceal it, thought her a traitor for being Christian. Obviously Jayanti and Khuku would disagree, their religion is of real importance and worth debating, something to be proudly claimed. Rupa can't imagine discussing the topic at all with any of her friends, let alone doing so with such ardor. She gently pushes Priya away so that she flops onto the bed where she pretends to be asleep.

Khuku's husband comes in from work. He stands in the doorway and glances round the room before uttering a few gruff words of greeting. He has the brittle manner of a man whose reserves have dried up, who has carried the weight of so much worry in his lifetime that there is no suppleness left in him. Like an egg he can go on supporting the load from above which is always with him, but if a blow came from the side he would crack. He hands his aluminium tiffin carrier to his wife, and takes the glass of water she offers, then fetches a cane stool and joins in the argument.

"And now Pope John Paul has made things much more difficult for us. Did you hear, did you hear what he said? He said the first thousand years since Jesus' birth brought Christianity to Europe, the next thousand years took it to Africa and America, and he hopes this next thousand years will see the growth of Christianity in Asia. He said that in the capital of India! Didn't he think what could happen to us?" He tilts his head emphatically, spreads the fingers of both hands into rounded bowls and shakes them vigorously, a prosaic version of the dancer's movements.

"Well it said in the paper that when he celebrated Mass the Jawaharlal Nehru Stadium was decorated with oil lamps because it's Diwali, and they included the arati ceremony in the service. They can't go further than that, can they?" cousin Khuku responds brightly.

Her husband ignores this interruption and continues in a voice suddenly grave, "He's an old man. He doesn't understand, but surely one of his party could have warned him, the Delhi Archbishop or someone. Why didn't anyone tell him how Hindu nationalists would react?" Rupa breathes in the odor of despair.

They walk home past Chhoto kaku's corner shop where Bijoy is trying to decide which biscuits to buy. He doesn't want to buy loose ones from the glass jars on the side shelves, but the ones in packets are in a cabinet at the back of the shop still in their plastic wrapping, so it isn't easy to choose. Standing on tiptoe he peers over the narrow counter trying to see past the weighing apparatus, piles of soap, hanging strips of washing powder sachets, batteries and brightly colored torches. Other customers and passers-by congregate on the wide step in front of the shop to inspect the children's newly arrived pishima with friendly interest. Rupa smiles and answers questions, flattered to be afforded celebrity status. When Jayanti grows impatient and orders Bijoy to hurry up, he obediently concludes his purchase.

Together they walk on, Bijoy clutching the biscuits to his chest, past houses where rows of tiny oil lamps and candles have been placed along the edges of verandas and roofs. Approaching on foot like this, Rupa notices that from the outside Sunil's house is a strange patchwork made up of bare brickwork still showing the holes where walls have been built round bamboo scaffolding, of roughly plastered surfaces, and of other areas which have been properly finished off with color wash. Showing the various stages of growth like the rings of a tree trunk, except that these are evident for all to see whereas the tree has to be destroyed before you can find out its history. You could read the family's financial fortunes in the various extensions and additions to the building, each corresponding to the maturing of an insurance or a lump sum payment of arrears. Dark blotches and greeny yellow streaks discolor the originally gray plaster, and the whole surface is covered with a fine web of cracks, depressing in its resemblance to the concrete of the council flats Rupa regularly visits, and rather incongruous here in a rural setting.

When they turn into the gateway Bijoy points to what looks like a solidified sack of cement, the pattern of woven threads from the long-rotted cloth is perfectly preserved. "Don't get too close," he warns gruffly, "it's dirty. Every dog that gets into the garden goes and pisses on that sack. My dad says it's become a territory marker."

As she goes up the stairs to wash her face, hands and feet and change her clothes, past the hen sitting eternally in its bowl, Rupa hears Nirmal babu say, "You see, you see! She's got a stomach pain and won't eat her food. I told you so, I told you dancing wasn't good for girls of her age."

Rupa remembers coming in unnoticed to see her mother's back bent over the sink or standing at the cooker, shoulders and wrists moving in tune with the tape that plays. A tilt of the head, shift of weight from foot to foot, ankles and toes – yes, Ma had been a dancer. What else had she given up by agreeing, or perhaps being forced, who knows, to marry? No it doesn't fit, this portrayal of Nirmal babu as a repressive husband. With Rupa he seems cold and with Priya strict, but with Bijoy, and yes with Chhaya also, he can be affectionate and tender. Perhaps the blame, if you can talk of blame, is on Ma's side.

The thought catches Rupa unawares and she shivers. Even to consider the possibility of Ma's "guilt" puts a distance between them, the separation slices through her. Is it like this when you discover your lover's been cheating on you, leading a parallel life about which you know nothing? The shared reality created by the two of you explodes suddenly and collapses. Not that Ma has betrayed her, of course not, it's just that their lives are so entwined. Ma doesn't try to hold her close, yet however physically far apart they are, each keeps the other in view, they breathe for each other.

Rupa realizes how naïve she's been, hoping to remain the detached investigator. This isn't about gathering information for a family history, recreating past events to put the record straight. She already knew the family could be disturbed by her questioning. It was this fear that troubled her, made her hesitant. When she and Jayanti talked earlier Rupa saw just how fragile was her sister's confidence, how easily the fallout from a determined search could damage her. What Rupa hasn't appreciated is the effect on her own feelings toward her parents, depending on what she discovers, and in consequence the effect on how she feels about herself.

> Laughter and tears   diamond and jade   this way
>   and that.
> Vibrating rhythm   weal and woe   beat by beat.

Rupa is never happy with opposites, with polarization. On or off, young or old, dead or alive, good or evil, black or white. Groups of three are more comfortable, offering a bit more room to maneuver, providing a middle position you can align with. Low, medium, high; cold, colder, coldest; red, amber, green; earth, sea, sky; past, present, future. Were her parents opposites, conflicting personalities, or complementary, falling in love after their marriage and fashioning a compromise, a comfortable middle position? Were their children born of passion or of habit? Rupa tries to imagine their young lives, but the evidence is too scanty.

CHAPTER FIVE
1960
ॐ

All night the kirtan parties displayed their skills, each group striving to outdo the others in emotional intensity, originality and zeal. At first Mary Featherstone sat with the crowds, watching and listening, sometimes joining in, sometimes moved almost to tears by the beauty and sincerity of words and music. She understood why they said attending one good kirtan performance was as beneficial as sitting through many sermons. She watched men and women capture the rhythm, swaying and clapping, interjecting shouts of approval and encouragement, joining in the chorus in voices sweet and gruff. One child, no more than two years old, rocked her whole body to the beat, on and on, oblivious to everything around her, totally absorbed in the song until her father took her in his lap, breaking the enchantment.

She always enjoyed this day, the Tuesday before the festival proper commenced. People began arriving in the afternoon, and the evening was spent in repentance and confession, spiritual preparation for the day itself. Then the singing started and continued with a life of its own, the music emerging naturally from the earlier mood of humility and the assurance of forgiveness, and continuing right through till the Wednesday morning.

Every town and village that had a few Christians produced its own kirtan party, often more than one. Singers accompanied by tabla and harmonium, flute and hand cymbals, violin and khol were eager to sing their own compositions or to perform their own variations on well-known numbers. Sometimes they formed two groups and sang responding verses alternately, sometimes the whole party sang in unison. Competitions were held and prizes awarded, and miraculously the customary quarrels and falling out did not happen, or if they did, were quickly settled. Later, on the Wednesday afternoon, the kirtan parties would progress through the village, each followed by groups of worshippers who sang until the air and sky resounded to their music. Villagers caught up in the joyful mood would walk behind them, and then watch as they reassembled at the festival ground still singing and often breaking into dance.

The festival was born in 1895 when a group of worshippers saw a dazzling light appear in their midst as they prayed together in Maliyapota village, and when they felt the church walls tremble, a sign to them of an outpouring of the Holy Spirit. Since then, on the first Wednesday following Ash Wednesday every year, the festival of Thanksgiving Wednesday had been celebrated in one of the villages in Nadia District, a different village each time depending on whose invitation the organizing committee decided to accept. All of the numerous Christian denominations participated, and many devout followers of other religious traditions too, those living nearby were attracted by the enthusiasm and excitement of the occasion, others came from further away on account of the reputation the festival had earned. City dwellers ate with farming folk, the educated and wealthy slept alongside laborers. Enormous pandals were erected and spread with straw for bedding, or used at mealtimes when row upon row of worshippers sat in front of large leaf-plates, waiting to be served whatever food had been prepared.

This morning Mary's head throbbed and her mouth tasted foul. Last night's food had been too highly spiced for her digestive system, but she could hardly expect her customary glass of hot water to be available here. One of the local Church leaders offered to let her sleep in his house and she accepted, reluctantly because to do so transgressed the festival's ideals, but as she grew older she found physical discomfort harder to bear. She hadn't actually slept much, partly because of the music, partly because the progressive fulfillment of her plan held her mind in a state of agitation. Nirmal Sarkar, who accompanied her, was also invited to take advantage of a little comfort, but he preferred to sleep in the pandal, perhaps wanting to keep some distance between the two of them. True, she was acting as an older relative in these marriage negotiations, but she was also his headmistress.

From where she sat on the veranda Mary could see people strolling round the village in pairs, gossiping and joking as they cleaned their teeth with twigs torn from a neem tree or from the castor oil bush hedges, or using their fingers dipped in ash collected from yesterday's cooking fire. She could smell smoke from one fire which had already been lit to heat water for the two thousand or more cups of tea which would be served, with dry biscuits and puffed rice, as refreshment after the early morning celebration of the Lord's Supper. That was when they had arranged to meet the girl's father, uncle and mother, and of course the girl herself. Thanksgiving Wednesday was used by many families as a convenient way of searching out eligible partners for their sons and daughters, and as an auspicious occasion on which to introduce prospective couples.

When her missionary colleague, who knew the family well, suggested this meeting place, Mary had no qualms about the propriety of it, just a tiny niggle about the incredible enthusiasm with which Nirmal received her initial suggestion. Was he rather too ardent, too completely caught up with the idea to be able to make a rational decision? She stretched her tall frame, spreading wide arms and legs, stood up to undo the strings attached to the corners of her mosquito net, tidied away her bedding, and gathering her washing things went cheerfully out to the pump in the yard, resolved to dispel her headache with good cheer, and her bad breath with Colgate.

The administration of the bread and wine to such a huge gathering took a very long while, but as always Mary was impressed by the orderly way in which the operation was managed, so different from the way in which they usually did things. All down to the Holy Spirit! Afterwards she and Nirmal walked together towards the point where tea was being distributed, but he was uncomfortable with the intimacy this implied, and fell back whenever her many acquaintances stooped to take the dust of her feet and share their latest news. She wasn't going to let him escape and each time drew him into the conversation, introducing him as one of her most able teachers. When two men approached and greeted her more formally, her lighthearted manner was at once transformed into an eager attentiveness.

"You must be Miss Featherstone, she said you would wait for us here. Let me introduce myself, I'm the girl's uncle and this is my elder brother – her father. We're so pleased to meet you today at this holy festival." The speaker pressed his hands together in namaskar, his expression one of genuine delight. The older man nodded politely. His features were sharp and neat, his manner controlled and dignified. So, he was the quiet one and he'd brought his younger brother to do the talking. She guessed they had arrived that morning since they certainly didn't look as if they'd spent the night lying on straw in a crowded pandal. Both wore dhoti and round necked shirts, newly washed and starched, and their hair was freshly oiled.

"Good, good, very good! You see me because I tall, very tall. This Nirmal Sarkar. He my very good friend. He teach in Mission School." As she turned to include him in the introductions Mary became aware they were attracting attention, a small group of curious onlookers was beginning to form. "We go private place? Come, then we talk, no one hear our talk." Her Bengali accent was poor, her grammar worse, but today this didn't seem to diminish her authority, rather it gave a special quality to her speech which fascinated the listeners.

The brothers sat side by side on a bench, the father upright with his legs crossed, the uncle leaning forward resting his arms on his thighs. Nirmal brought a chair for Mary which she acknowledged with humorously exaggerated courtesy, then placed his own stool near the two men. Mother and daughter sat coyly at the other end of the veranda, listening intently to every word.

"I must start by telling you this; we've joined in this festival for six years now, ever since my nephew, Poltu, was cured of a chronic stomach complaint by the padre's prayers. It's never mattered to us what religion our friends are, my father used to invite all kinds of people to our house and, as boys, encouraged us to do the same. So we were excited when Thanksgiving Wednesday was held in our village, especially as we heard there would be a gathering at midday for curing of the sick. What did we do? We took Poltu along – he wasn't keen to begin with but we insisted – and when the padre laid his hands on the boy's head a miracle happened! Truly, a miracle! Now he's very strong and in good health, his wife has come to live with us and he's learning his father's trade, and we have to fulfil the vow we made. So that's the reason we've come here to meet you today."

The uncle's delivery was animated, with generous use of hand gestures and frequent appeals to his brother for confirmation of his account, appeals which were met with minimal jerks of the head. As if to compensate for this, Mary responded to each stage of the tale with lively expressions of interest and surprise. She'd heard the story from her friend and had already communicated it to Nirmal, but she appreciated the uncle's need to rehearse it in front of the combined parties as a prelude to later negotiations.

"Of course we always contribute to the festival costs, they'll take a collection later this morning, I expect you know that. We give as generously as we can, but there is also the vow to fulfil. My brother promised to give one of his daughters to a Christian boy. You understand why? I'll tell you. It was at this Christian festival that his son was cured, so in return he'll give his daughter to a Christian family."

From the far end of the veranda the mother interrupted, but her dialect was too obscure for Mary to catch what she said, so the girl's uncle interpreted. "She says we only want a good boy. That's why we asked the memsahib, we trusted her to choose someone from a good family."

When the mother spoke, Nirmal turned towards the two women and continued to look in their direction, and for the first time Mary also looked at them properly. The girl's body was wholly covered by her pale pink sari, which was the color of fresh rose buds and delicately traced with silver threads. Her hair was caught up in a large bun from which a few curly strands strayed, but

65

she kept her head down so that her face was hidden in shadow. Although she was still very young, as far as Mary could judge she already had the well-formed figure appreciated by Indians. The mother's teeth and gums were red from chewing pan (another disgusting habit involving spitting), but her beaming face returned Mary's look with open warmth as she waggled her head encouragingly from side to side.

As if by common consent everyone's attention then turned to Nirmal, even the girl glanced quickly at his face before lowering her head again. He hesitated, apparently not sure of the protocol, and looked to Mary for guidance. Not one to pay attention to social protocol even if she'd been familiar with it, Mary confidently launched into a description of Nirmal's circumstances and good character, enthusiastically recommending him as an excellent future son-in-law. Finally she gestured to him, "You say, Nirmal, say about yourself."

"I'm sincerely grateful to Miss Featherstone for arranging this meeting, and to you all for coming here today, and hope you will not be disappointed. As my parents are sadly both deceased and my uncle is in poor health and therefore unable to travel, Miss Featherstone has taken upon herself the responsibility of finding for me a girl who will share my life – its joys and sorrows. I know that although you are a Hindu family you wish to marry your daughter to a Christian boy, and I am very happy to hear it. However, I must make it clear that my wife would have to become a Christian wholeheartedly, she must take instruction in all aspects of my religion, and of course be baptized. Then I would cherish her forever and promise to be a loving husband." Mary was so proud of the measured gravity with which Nirmal delivered this speech, of the direct and simple way in which he made his position clear. His last words were accompanied by a sudden shy smile, which lightened the effect.

The girl's father must also have been impressed by Nirmal's declaration, for he in turn began to explain that his family originated in East Bengal, East Pakistan that is, where he had worked as a first-class craftsman, designing and manufacturing high quality gold ornaments. All the wealthy families had ordered jewelry for their wives and daughters from his shop. Then ten years ago he and his brother decided to move to West Bengal because of the political situation, the gold trade was always amongst the first businesses to be adversely effected by political disturbances, but it had been a struggle to establish himself here. He was finding it difficult to build up a reputation and his business was not doing particularly well. Mary had the uncharitable thought that this lack of prosperity might have as much bearing on their plan to choose a Christian boy, as had their purported vow; she'd heard dowry demands these days were incredibly high. Then he turned to his wife and suggested they let their daughter answer any questions put to her. The mother vigorously nodded her assent, and nudged the girl.

Mary inquired how far she had studied, what her hobbies were, whether or not she knew how to cook. Standard questions and therefore hopefully the ones for which she was prepared, Mary had no wish to catch her out or embarrass her. The girl met Mary's eyes and answered in a clear voice, although her rapid breathing indicated how nervous she felt. When Nirmal asked whether she understood what he said earlier, she replied she did, and that she was ready to accept his conditions. She said she'd already heard some Bible stories from her friend, and was eager to learn more. Mary saw the look on his face and knew he was captivated, head over heels in love, irrevocably hooked. She had to admit that the girl handled the whole situation admirably, and her appearance – she was blessed with a combination of her father's well-defined features and her mother's open expression – was as pleasing as her manner.

Later Mary sat in the Thanksgiving meeting amidst a gathering so large that those on the outskirts were forced to stand under the trees. One by one they gave thanks for exams passed, family feuds resolved, employment secured, businesses revived, recovery from illness. Her own heart was full of the blessings for which she offered her deepest gratitude. It couldn't have gone more smoothly, they were all of one mind over the arrangements for the marriage, leaving only some minor details still to be settled. Then Nirmal would bring his bride back to his quarters at the

Mission School, he'd have to move into married quarters naturally but that shouldn't pose a problem, and the other staff would be transformed by her unexpected presence. They would take care of her, teach and guide her, and in so doing find their own true spiritual strength.

That night there would be a great feast, open to all whether or not they had participated in the festival, when those who lived daily with hunger could fill their stomachs tight. She'd heard it said the leftovers kept the local dogs satisfied for three or four days afterwards, their barking was their own thanksgiving.

CHAPTER SIX

Mary had invited George Koshy to her room so that together they could work out the final details of the timetable for the next school year, and, always one to mix business with pleasure, she prepared afternoon tea, scones and fruitcake. She was delighted with the texture of the scones, beautifully light. In place of the ground almonds required by the cake recipe she used chickpea flour, a trick she'd often heard of but never tried before, and substituted peanuts for walnuts – much cheaper. Everything was arranged prettily on fine china plates so they could take as much or as little as required, a system she much preferred to their habit of serving individual plates already made up, each with its allotted portion. So wasteful, unless you happened to be hungry, and then so mean. She must remember to put sugar on the tray and an extra teaspoon, teapot and hot water jug, although they never accepted a second cup once it had been watered down.

She saw George walk past the kitchen door and called to him cheerily, saying she was on her way. He stopped, came back, and offered to carry the tray into her room where she indicated the table she'd already positioned to receive it. He sat uncomfortably on a cane stool, while she knelt beside Captain Featherstone's trunk on which sheets of paper were spread ready for their work on the timetable, or "routine," as they insisted on calling it. His eyes moved nervously between the papers and the tea tray.

"Don't worry, Mr. Koshy, this is just a draft, it's not going to matter if it gets crumbs or jam on it," she laughed. "We'll leave the tea to brew a while. I've begun to fill in some parts – English Comprehension and Composition, Maths, Moral Science – class teachers can teach those subjects themselves in the junior school. But the South Indian staff shouldn't be taking their own Hindi lessons, and we wanted to use the youth volunteer from Cambridge for Craft this year didn't we, because he has ideas and enthusiasm." She thought with frustration of the easels, paints (probably dried up by now) and colored paper which she'd brought back from her last furlough, but which had never been touched. They just didn't have the imagination, all they ever did was copy someone else's drawing.

She poured the tea, passed him the plates of scones and cake, and then they began to study the timetable seriously. George Koshy couldn't get close enough to the trunk to see clearly on account of his knees which stuck out awkwardly, and his cumbersome feet which obstructed his efforts. What ugly feet he had, a tuft of hair springing out from the joint of each bulbous toe, heels sloping outwards like an elephant's. As a child he was probably a dear little specimen, Mary had always thought the passing from boy to manhood a tragedy. There was something offensive about those naked male feet in her room, but she must try to concentrate on the timetable. They worked hard for two hours, juggling with rooms and staff abilities, with science and sports equipment and sets of textbooks, till they finally copied out an individual "routine" for each teacher and each class.

Before he left, Mary wanted to gauge George's opinion of Nirmal's marriage, of the effectiveness of her idea and plan. She wanted to hear him acknowledge her project to be a success. She sat back on the floor, long legs tucked under her with her skirt spread over them.

"They seem to be doing alright, don't they, the newly weds? Nirmal and his bride I mean. They're obviously besotted with one another. She mixes with the lady teachers, comes to evening prayers, appears to be quite at home here. And the other staff are responding well, overall I'd say there's been a marked improvement, wouldn't you? They're all taking their responsibilities more seriously, the whole atmosphere in school's been pleasanter these last few months." She fixed her pale blue eyes intently on him. *Now are you going to tell me honestly what you think, or disagree deliberately just for the sake of it?*

George looked down at his hands, bending back the fingers of each hand in turn, and making little throat clearing noises as he considered his reply. "Nirmal Sarkar is working as hard as ever, I do not think his changed family circumstances have distracted him at all from his duties. I could not really say much about his wife, I have not had any occasion to speak with her as she is not a member of staff, but I have heard of no difficulties." Although he had stopped speaking she could sense there was more to come. She wouldn't help him out, he'd have to do it by himself. "I do, however, feel you should have discussed this with me, as your Deputy and future Principal of the school, before the marriage took place. I should be consulted on all matters involving members of staff. I was deeply hurt by your failure to include me in your plans."

Mary hadn't expected this but would have to hear him out, after all she had asked. "What would you have said if I had asked your opinion?" Her voice was tight and hard and she was ashamed of the anger and the resentment she felt. She should be able to accept criticism from a colleague, with good grace.

"I would have asked you to consider why you wanted to arrange this marriage. Did you consider it the best thing for Nirmal Sarkar or for the school, *your* school as you like to call it? I would have asked if it was right to use one couple for the purpose of improving the morale of an institution. And then I would have asked you to think of the difference in age and background between the bride and groom, and of the future of this couple once they become a family."

She was so surprised that she stood up and stacked the timetable papers into a neat pile, in order to give herself time to recover. Her hands were unsteady. Having cleared a space, she sat down on the trunk.

"It's ridiculous to call what I've done interfering! You know very well marriages are arranged all the time, that's how things are done here. Usually by relatives, yes, but Nirmal's parents are both dead, and his uncle was happy for me to go ahead. He's thirty-five for goodness sake, hardly a child, he can make his own decisions, and he was absolutely in favor of the proposal." No, she was not going to accept this censure from him, she had not gone into this rashly, on the contrary she had proceeded with careful thought and much prayer.

"I admit the age gap is more than I would have liked, but it means she'll have the strength to look after the household and the children when he's busy with school work, and still be young enough to take care of him in his old age." Those weren't lame excuses, they were the standard arguments offered when the girl was much younger than the boy – fifteen years younger was nothing out of the ordinary in this country. "And, yes, I do think it's sometimes justifiable to think in community rather than individual terms, I'd have thought that was typical of Indian society. But anyway no one's interests have been sacrificed, two people have been made very happy and at the same time the school has benefited. I refuse to accept there's anything wrong in that."

"I understand your defence but I do not agree with it, and hope you will not later regret your actions. I acknowledge we have had a successful and relatively peaceful few months at school, but there is no justification for attributing that to Nirmal Sarkar's marriage. Thank you for your hard work on the timetable, it is a complicated matter but I think we have been successful in sorting it out. I will see you in school tomorrow for the admission tests."

George Koshy stood up awkwardly and knocked the pile of papers with his knee so that they slid onto the floor, from where he tried to gather them up, crumpling them as he did so. Mary bent down quickly to help, which brought her into proximity to those distasteful feet again, and cheerfully reassured him that no damage had been done. Not to the timetable at least, she thought, her pride and self-confidence on the other hand were certainly in need of repair.

After his departure Mary went into the kitchen to heat the

milk on the electric ring, so it wouldn't go off before morning. Twice she let the froth rise to the top of the pan before removing it from the heat and placing it, still steaming hot, in the little food cupboard for the night. As she fastened the padlock on the wire mesh door she glanced up to see Nirmal in the doorway. He smiled at her, and at her invitation came in to sit at the dining table where she joined him. She shook her head in mock despair and laughed.

"It's good to see you, Nirmal, you don't seem to have time to make social calls on me nowadays. I wonder why?" He didn't mind the teasing, in fact he rather enjoyed it, and laughed back, "You of all people should know why that is!" It restored a balance to her opinion of men, chatting in this relaxed way with Nirmal. They talked for a while about how each had spent the Christmas holiday, and she inquired about his uncle's state of health. He asked her advice about one of his students who was both very intelligent and very funny, a born comic who had the class in stitches whenever he was in trouble. He said he found it easy enough to discipline a naughty or lazy student, but one who always had the class on his side because he was so entertaining, that was another matter. She made a number of suggestions and offered to have a word with the boy herself. It was late and Mary wanted to get to bed, but Nirmal showed no signs of leaving.

"Is everything alright with your wife? She seems to be settling in very well, she's a lovely girl. How are the Bible lessons going? It's Mr. Das who teaches her isn't it?" This should give him an opening to talk about more personal matters if that was what he wanted.

"She's wonderful! I've never been so happy in my entire life. You chose just the right person for me, Miss Featherstone, she makes my life complete. That sounds sentimental, but it's true. When I come home in the evening after giving tuitions, I can hear her singing even before I open the door. And in the morning there she is beside me, my wife waking up with a smile." And after a brief silence during which she waited expectantly, "I wanted to give you some news …"

"Oh, congratulations! My goodness, that was quick. I am

delighted, absolutely delighted! When is it due?" She leant over and placed her hand momentarily on his arm to convey the depth of her emotion. He smiled back and she noticed there were tears in his eyes, so she stood up and went over to the electric ring on which she'd just heated the milk, pretending to check that it was switched off.

"We are both very happy about it, very happy indeed, but there is one thing which worries me now. My wife has hinted she'd like to go back to her mother's house when the baby's due, and stay with her family for a month or so. I wouldn't feel at all happy about letting her go. We do things differently from them, and I want my child to begin in the right way, do you understand? We visited her family together during the holidays and they treated me very well, cooked three different kinds of fish and brought loads of curds and sweets in my honor. They expected us to stay the night but I refused. We went home to my uncle the same evening. I think that disappointed her, well I know it did, and probably offended them as well. And now she's planning to go to her mother for the confinement, and it's worrying me very much. I don't want to upset her, everything around her should be peaceful at this time, but if I say nothing she'll be even more hurt later when I do forbid her to go." He looked up anxiously, his eyes pleading with her to find him a way out, some wise advice that would resolve his dilemma.

Mary was glad to be on the other side of the room so he couldn't read her expression. For the second time that afternoon she was startled by what she heard. Whereas she had known just how to refute George's outburst, Nirmal's words left her undecided, a frame of mind she rarely experienced. She sympathized with his reservations about his wife returning to her parents for any length of time, especially for such an important event, yet she also understood the girl's desire to be with her mother. With the one person who would know just what to do, just how to encourage and reassure her, and of course it was their custom for the wife to go to her father's house for her first delivery. If Nirmal's mother were alive it would be easier, or even an aunt, but there was no one, no female relative apart from his sister and she was not long married herself. A terrible doubt hovered just out of focus on the edge of Mary's thoughts, and she turned firmly away from it.

"She must have the baby here, and her mother can come and live here for a few weeks to take care of everything. Don't worry, I'll clear it with Mr. Koshy."

CHAPTER SEVEN
1999

Earlier in the year Sunil gave Bijoy a small patch of ground for his own. With his father's help Bijoy dug over the ground, removed the stones and rubbish, then put up a fence of sticks and small branches to protect the plot against dogs and chickens. He collected the long black seeds with straw like tufts from dried up marigold flowers and scattered them over the soil, ruffling the surface with his finger tips until the seeds were covered.

He carried water from the pump in an old hair oil bottle and dribbled it over the seeds, and watched every day until the first signs of life appeared, two pale narrow leaves on a pale red stem, like outspread hands on delicate wrists. Later these turned darker green and darker red, and looked like wings stretching upward as if they longed to fly. The next set of leaves had serrated edges like the edges of his mother's hand-fan. Priya and her friends planned to use the flowers to make garlands, but Bijoy would rather leave them on the plants.

When Sunil said the plants were strong enough, Bijoy took a small blunt trowel and loosened the soil along the border of the garden on both sides of the gate, then gently dug up the seedlings, and taking care to protect the fragile roots with his small hands, replanted them in two evenly spaced rows. Now tight hard buds have formed, and Bijoy waits impatiently for them to open. One evening he brings Priya to show her a few buds which have lengthened and grown loose and soft, with scraps of gold appearing at the mouth, so nearly open they must surely blossom the next day. The anticipation wakes him early, but when Bijoy reaches the plants he sees that the flowers have been torn off and taken away. This happens again on the next three mornings, even though he comes outside before going to the bathroom or washing his face.

Now his tears are shed more in anger than sorrow and each time he remains sullen the whole day, preoccupied with plans to catch the culprit. He guesses of course that the flowers are being taken to offer in puja, but he hasn't actually seen anyone stealing them. When his school van passes Haldar babu's wife walking along the lane away from Bijoy's house, bearing a heap of marigold flowers in her cupped hands, he is convinced some of those flowers are from his garden, and vows to take revenge.

After the midday meal he lies quiet and still beside his mother, waiting for her to fall asleep. Chhaya has spent all morning washing clothes so Bijoy hopes she's tired and will doze off quickly. He slowly lifts his head, just enough to see his mother's mouth has fallen slightly open, and to check the even rise and fall of her shoulder beneath the damp hair spread out over the pillow. Holding his breath and taking care to keep all his movements slow and smooth, he eases himself out from under the light cover and half slides half rolls off the bed. His bare feet make no sound on the hard floor, he feels the grittiness of the morning's dust underfoot as he moves toward the door of Nirmal babu's room.

Bijoy moves with a quiet determination, each action planned and premeditated. He can hear jagged snoring coming from the pile of clothes and papers on the bed. With his eyes fixed on the sleeping mound – his grandfather – he creeps toward the bench under which the walking stick lies. The walking stick with the silver-plated knob given by Sunil last Christmas and received with a grunt, which has lain under the bench ever since. It has to be this walking stick, nothing else is long enough. Bijoy has experimented with the sweeping broom and various kitchen utensils but none will do, only the pole for plucking ripe fruit off the tree is long enough to reach, but it's too long for him to carry. He hopes too that some of Nirmal babu's authority will be transferred to his actions through the walking stick.

He stoops and fumbles under the bench, carefully feeling each object to check if it's what he's searching for, but ready to draw back his hand at once if it touches something revolting. It's too dark down there to see, so he only has his fingers to work with, trying to be quick but silent, and all the while his neck is craned so he can keep his eyes flitting between the snoring hump on the bed and the door to his mother's room. At last he finds the smooth polished curve of the walking stick and gently extracts it from the jumble of objects under the bench. The mosquitoes which live in the dark places are disturbed and fly sleepily around biting his ankles, but he can't slap them because of the noise, so has to suffer the discomfort.

When Bijoy reaches the veranda he uses the end of his vest to wipe the cobwebs from the dark wood, and rubs the silver-plating against his shorts. He climbs onto the iron bed and tugs his blue shirt off the line, struggling to force his arms through damp sleeves. His outdoor shoes aren't on the step where they should be and this disturbs his concentration, instead he slides his feet defiantly into his house-wearing sandals. The final preparation is a comb pulled through his thick curls. The mirror tells him this will do and he goes down the steps and passes the pump where he longs to rinse his fingers clear of clinging cobweb traces but can't risk the creaking sound. Placing the walking stick under his arm, Bijoy walks round to the gate and into the lane.

At midday the lanes are deserted. Those who work have been away since morning, and those who don't have eaten heavily and are idle. Doors are closed and curtains drawn against the light, and prying eyes. A dog lies curled, its rubbery tail twisted up by its ears, its coat sandy-gray and moth-eaten. Bijoy has no expression on his face, just the mechanical look of a clockwork toy which must go on until the coil has unwound. He doesn't notice the dog and it ignores him, he does hear a cycle-bell approach from behind and changes track ever so slightly to allow it to pass him on the narrow lane. Usually he would glance at the rider with curiosity to see if it was someone he knows, but today he keeps his eyes ahead, the walking stick firm in his armpit, his feet moving step by step in his house sandals. A loose flapping accompanies each step as his heel lifts off the ground and up in the air before the sandal can catch up. Then the heel lands on the sandal again slopping to one side, only the thong between the toes holding it in place.

He reaches the first corner, passing Chhoto kaku's shop with its single blue wooden eyelid firmly closed. The brick cabin has half a roof, from the ridge it slopes down only one way. The building looks unfinished, as if the other slope and the other eye were intended but have been forgotten. The shade, a thick concrete slab topped with corrugated iron, sticks out abruptly over the shop front, forlorn now that there are no customers for it to shelter. It can't fold itself and rest in the heat of the day like the solitary shuttered eye, which sleeps until late afternoon when children will be sent to buy tea leaves and loose biscuits. The shade has no choice but to continue protruding absurdly. An abandoned ricksha van loaded with empty cooking gas cylinders, rests at an angle against the wall of the shop. At the sides of the lane lies a dusty accumulation of broken stems, broken pottery, paper bags and torn strips of plastic.

The muscles of Bijoy's upper arm are beginning to ache, he is pressing the walking stick so tightly into his armpit. Now he is walking in the shadows keeping close to the bamboo fence of Haldar babu's house, or rather his land because the house is set well back from the lane with a large yard in front of it. Along the line of the bamboo poles a few trees have been planted and the hanging leaves scratch Bijoy's face as he walks, more cautiously and lightly now. He lets the walking stick slip down into his hand as he nears the opening in the boundary fence, who knows, it might be needed for protection. There's no gate, but crossing into Haldar babu's land from the lane feels like going through a barrier more real than any gate. The air, the ground underfoot, the quietness, the light, are quite different inside someone else's territory, someone's space where he shouldn't be and where he has only one purpose.

Just inside the entrance an area has been laid with bricks to stop the ground from turning to mud in the rainy season. Beyond that the dusty ground is swept clean, a vast clear space between where Bijoy stands and the house, occupied only by one small building – the thakur-ghor, the room where an image of the family god or goddess is kept. In front of this room is a shade supported by pillars painted pink, green and gold, an elegant shade molded at the front into a scalloped archway. Under the shade a highly polished platform extends beyond the room, dropping down to a wide lower step, so that you have to approach the thakur-ghor itself by stages. Here, every Saturday, there are kirtan parties. Old men and women gather with drums and bells, and chant and sing and wail and ululate, and in his house Nirmal babu complains and wails his own hymns specially loud to blot out the noise. Now nothing moves and there is little sound, except for the occasional breathy snort from the cattle tethered behind the house out of sight.

Keeping firm hold of his grandfather's walking stick Bijoy crosses to the solitary room, and crouches down on the side hidden from the house. He doesn't look at the house but in his imagination can see Haldar babu's wife coming down the steps wearing a plain house sari, stretching the afternoon sleep out of her thin body, her loose uncombed hair straggling round her shoulders. A pale blue metal grill covers the wide doorway of the thakur ghor, but when he puts his face close against the grill Bijoy can see into the dark interior. Round the walls hang faded pictures: Radha Krishna entranced by his flute, Durga resplendent on her lion, and the diaphanous duo Nimai and Nitai, arms uplifted. A cord coming from the ceiling where it is attached to a bell, hangs in the middle of the room.

At the back he can see the darkly carved wooden shrine surrounded by tiny brass dishes, jars, candles, a conch shell, a grinding stone spattered with sandalwood paste, a book on a stand, and other remains of the midday puja. And flowers. The white jasmine flowers arranged along the front of the shrine and strewn here and there over plates and vessels show up clearly in the gloom, he can also see the orange of marigolds, dimly glowing at the feet of the goddess.

Bijoy stares at the goddess and sticks out his tongue, right out as far as it will go, in imitation and mockery of Kali. But this image is not Kali. She wears a golden headdress, and a number of garlands softly shimmering in the gloom, decorate her neck. Orange flowers have been tucked into one hand and into the folds of her sari, marigolds from his own garden. Bijoy's tongue goes out again and he whispers a word he has heard Sunil say under his breath when he thinks no one is listening.

Then Bijoy takes the walking stick, pokes it through the grill, holding it by the silver plated knob, and slowly stretches his arm as far as he can reach. The walking stick touches the wooden shrine and a brass pot is dislodged. It rolls silently in a curve and stops at the goddess's feet. Bijoy adjusts his grip so that he is holding the silver knob with only his fingertips, and lunging forward he strikes the goddess so that she wobbles and then falls on her side. The movement is so sudden and forceful that the walking stick shoots out of his hand and he can't pick it up again.

He springs up, swivels round, and dashes back through the gateway, along the lane, head down, breathing fast, arms and legs propelling him forward. First one then the other sandal flies off into the scrub. The cycle brakes only just in time. The startled dog jumps to its feet whining. He's sweating now and near to tears. No one is about in the front yard as he runs past the pump towards the mango tree. He can hear someone opening the veranda grills but doesn't turn to look. Stretching his arms wide and curling his toes to get a good grip, Bijoy climbs the tree. Sobbing, he pulls himself up, the bark rough and familiar on his palms and soles. He rests his face against the trunk, pressing the roughness into his cheek. Each time he pulls himself into a higher branch, his breathing hurts a little less.

Between sleeping and waking Rupa's brain struggles to hold the two states together, stitching them into one another using the methods her brain would have used when fully awake, but now with a strange irrationality. Her conscious mind tries to blend the fanciful scenes still blowing about her sleep-filled thoughts, with the stimuli from the outside world which have woken her. She and Jayanti and Ma (Rupa knows it's Ma although she looks much older and is attired in a white widow's sari), are shut in a small dark room where they dance in a frenzied and demented manner. Rupa is exhausted and begs to be allowed to stop for breath, but Ma urges her on. Through cracks in the window shutters Rupa can see a band of men approaching, led by Nirmal babu. They pound the shutters with clenched fists, all the time shouting at Ma to come out. And then the balance tips towards Rupa's waking consciousness, and she realizes that the sound of angry voices is coming up from the yard below.

She slides off the bed and keeping close to the wall peers out over the grills, moving slowly so as not to attract attention. From above the figures are distorted, faces are partly hidden but hand gestures and other movements are exaggerated. They have grouped in front of the veranda but have not climbed the steps. Two men wearing only lungi and vest are at the center of the action, and one of them has a stick which he repeatedly holds up, displaying it rather than using it aggressively. Other men and women stand round watching with various degrees of animation. Some nod and sway in sympathy with the two leaders, others remain detached observers. All the time newcomers are joining the edges of the group, women carrying babies and dragging toddlers, teenage boys who wheel their cycles round the pump and lean them against the mango tree so that they can get closer to see what is going on. Hands reach up to slide the hanging clothes which are obstructing the view to the far ends of the drying line, and one boy stands on the solid bag of cement to get a better look. Separate conversations start up in the crowd, so that everyone has to raise their voice to be heard.

Rupa can't recognize the two men but they are obviously very agitated, and their anger is directed at someone on the veranda. The voice from the veranda is kept under control so that she can't make out who is speaking, either Chhaya or Nirmal babu, surely neither Jayanti nor Sunil will have returned home yet? The dispute seems to concern damage to the image of some goddess, and the need for retribution. It doesn't make any sense to Rupa but she is worried by the mounting tension and steadily growing number of people who join the crowd. The yard is quite full now and people are beginning to fill the gaps under the trees, Rupa is afraid that as people are pressed together tempers will become more volatile. She feels a rising panic because she can't assess the situation, can't read the signs as she could have done at home. Then she sees the crowd make way for a figure in a blue and white school sari which pushes its way through to the front, and quickly disappears into the veranda.

Footsteps hurry up the steps and run to where Rupa is standing. Priya is excited, breathing rapidly, she wipes the sweat from her upper lip and forehead with the loose end of her sari, grimacing as she does so because the heavily starched cotton is rough and scratches her skin. Her eyebrows are raised in query as she looks at Rupa for reassurance. Rupa puts a strong arm around her niece's shoulders, disguising how inadequate she actually feels in the role of comforter.

"Don't worry, Priya, it'll be alright. They've only been here about ten minutes, I don't know what it's about. Who's talking to them, do you know those two at the front? Can you understand what's happening?" Priya is much more likely to make sense of it all than she is.

"The tall one is Haldar babu, you know who lives round the corner in the big house and has noisy kirtan parties on Saturday nights. And that's his son-in-law holding the stick. Oh! It's Dadu's stick. How did they get that? Rupa pishi, what's going to happen? Look, now they're shouting at my mother." Priya's excitement is turning to fear. There is absolutely nothing Rupa can do. She senses that for her to appear downstairs would probably do more harm than good.

There is a sudden lull in the commotion. They see Haldar babu and his son-in-law offer respectful greeting to someone on the veranda, and conclude that Nirmal babu must have come out of his room to speak with them. His voice can be clearly heard inviting them to come inside, and the two men climb the steps and disappear from sight. The crowd remains quiet. Some turn to inspect the aviary where Sunil keeps his love birds, cockatiels, canaries and finches. A woman crouches down and shoves her crying baby's head under her sari. Little children venture deeper into the garden and hide behind trees. Someone operates the pump while his friend drinks. Priya's pleasure at sharing this vantage point with Rupa returns, her face breaks into a conspiratorial grin.

"Shall we go down and listen to what they're saying?" Priya's bright eyes urge Rupa to share her curiosity, begging her not to behave like an adult.

Sitting half way down the stairs they can hear Haldar babu's agitated explanation of how his wife found the walking stick inside their thakur-ghor, and how she recognized it as belonging to Nirmal babu. The stick was found lying near the fallen image and must have been the instrument with which it was knocked over, but who did it and why? Haldar babu insists that one of Nirmal babu's family must be responsible, and demands to know who committed the outrage. Surely they don't suspect one of the adults? Well no, probably not. That leaves the children. Priya has just returned from school, they saw her come in, so it can't be her. Then what about Bijoy? Yes, Nirmal babu admits reluctantly, it could have been the boy, he must be called and interrogated.

"Bijoy isn't at home. When I woke up he had gone, and I can't find him. He's not at his friend's house either, I've checked." Chhaya's voice is calm and matter-of-fact. Priya looks at Rupa in alarm.

Haldar babu is triumphant, that proves Bijoy is the guilty one! Without giving him the chance to defend himself he shouldn't be condemned, but yes it does look likely. However, if it was the boy, then his grandfather thinks he can guess the reason behind the action. Nirmal babu explains about Bijoy and his flower garden, how carefully he tends his plants and how every day some flowers are stolen. Then Haldar babu says that if this is so, he can appreciate the child's anger. Still, the boy was wrong to do what he did and should be punished. Somewhat grudgingly he apologizes if his wife or daughter-in-law has taken Bijoy's flowers, it's true, they do collect flowers daily, he doesn't know where from. A third voice, probably the son-in-law, says something about the goddess wanting retribution, and Haldar babu tells him curtly to shut up. The voices continue for some time, Nirmal babu emphasizing that Bijoy is very young, the same age as Haldar babu's own grandson, Haldar babu stressing how devotedly his wife cares for the image in their thakur-ghor. Then, from the unevenness of his voice, Priya and Rupa can tell that Nirmal babu is getting up and is moving towards the veranda again. They hurry back upstairs, eager to observe what will happen next.

Priya hangs over the grills no longer caring who sees her, while the two elderly men stand together on the top step. Nirmal babu explains to everyone what has happened and says a few weighty words about them all being Bengali brothers, and that this unites them more strongly than their religious differences divide. Those watching begin to feel bored by the whole affair, the excitement has drained away. Rupa marvels at Nirmal babu's diplomacy, at his ability to judge the situation and control it so effectively. But she is a little skeptical of his liberal sentiments in view of his usual opinions about Hindus, and looks away out over the garden. She sees children playing near the beehives, and wonders whether she should go and warn them of the danger of being stung. Then a movement in the mango tree catches her eye. A pale blue movement, just enough to cause the leaves to tremble. She stares at the spot and can distinguish a patch of pale blue cloth from Bijoy's shirt. She puts a hand on Priya's arm and indicates with her eyes the exact place in the tree. Priya follows her eyes and catches her breath.

The crowd drifts away, disappointed at the anticlimax. One or two women pause to discuss the episode with Chhaya, and a few children remain engrossed in their game of hide and seek. Chhaya reaches up to spread the drying clothes out along the line once more.

Bijoy only comes down from the tree when Priya begs him to, he won't listen to his parents' pleading or to Jayanti and Nirmal babu's commands. That night he refuses to have his meal until his sister promises to serve his food and sit with him while he eats. Between mouthfuls he mutters, "Did you hear Dadu say we are all Bengali brothers? He's a hypocrite! He doesn't really think that. He's always saying they are Hindus and we are

Christians, they won't do anything for us and we shouldn't mix too much with them. Jesus didn't like hypocrites."

Chhaya is in the kitchen cooking the rooti which Rupa rolls out for her. She gives her son a severe look and warns him in a whisper to be quiet. Priya giggles and catches Rupa's eye, raising her eyebrows as she tilts her head slightly to one side, meaning "but he's right, isn't he?"

That night after family prayers, when Nirmal babu goes off to lie under his mosquito net, surrounded by papers and torches and clocks and his little tins stuffed with things that one day might be useful, Rupa wonders what the others think, whether they would call him a hypocrite.

"Never mind hypocrisy, I was very relieved when he decided to join in. Whatever he really believes, the situation was becoming quite dangerous and I think he did exactly what was needed. They respect him, and he used that respect to calm everyone down," Chhaya is clearly more shaken by the experience than Rupa has appreciated.

"Of course it wasn't dangerous!" Sunil looks amused, "Haldar babu sits on a panchayat committee with me. He bought land here the same time as we did, we shared our building tools with him. His grandson travels with Bijoy in the school van. He's not going to cause trouble just because a little boy knocks over one of the images in his thakur-ghor. He was annoyed that's all, or more likely his wife told him to come here. That's what happened, she's the one behind it. I'll go and talk to him in the morning, and perhaps I'll take Bijoy with me and get him to apologize."

Chhaya's imperceptible frown reveals her displeasure, but it is Rupa who speaks. "Listen, Sunil dada, she's right, it was turning nasty. Just imagine! Poor Chhaya boudi, trying to understand what they were talking about and at the same time wondering where Bijoy had got to. But she stayed calm, and listened carefully so that they felt she was taking their complaint seriously. I think she managed amazingly well."

"Okay, okay. I agree, Chhaya coped very well. But I don't believe there was ever any real danger." It is Sunil's way of handling conflict, agree with the other but reassert your own position, so that everyone's left feeling reasonably content. Rupa guesses he is well used to employing this strategy.

"And I don't think Baba is a hypocrite, whatever that means. Of course he thinks we are all Bengali and that ties us close together, we all think that." Sunil's admiration for his father is evident. "Privately he can believe that only Christians will be saved, will go to heaven, but that doesn't stop him continuing to live decently with Hindus. He doesn't have to say it publicly that's all. No civilized person wants trouble."

Jayanti comes out of the kitchen, stooping slightly while she dries her hands on the pleats of her sari. She sits on the iron bed and picks up the local newspaper. "Well then Sunil dada, tell me, was it okay for Padre babu to say during his sermon last Sunday that the Orissa cyclone was sent by God in punishment for the killing, the cruel burning, of the Australian missionary and his two sons? Because it was just Christians listening does that mean it was private? Or was it public because it was outside his own home?" Sunil is momentarily unsure of himself and doesn't reply.

Jayanti continues, "It's not a question of thinking one thing but being careful never to say it openly. Bijoy's right, that's hypocrisy. You've got to stop even thinking like that. You've got to forget about this 'who's going to be saved?' thing. Be a Christian definitely, but change some bits of your religion, let them grow a bit, to fit in with what's happening in the world. People have always done that."

Chhaya is quick to respond. "How on earth can Baba stop believing what he's always known to be true? He doesn't wake up and decide what to believe each day you know, like choosing what to wear and what to eat. He really does think only Christians know God fully, and whether you think that's arrogant or not I don't see how you can expect him to deny what he knows in his heart. So the only way for him is to have a public and a private face." She speaks with quiet passion.

"'Our staff reporter has received news from a small town in Kerala where one Catholic priest was assaulted and two church buildings suffered damage in arson attacks. The disturbances are thought to be part of an outbreak of anti-Catholic sentiment in the wake of the Pope's comments reported in this paper last week.'" Jayanti holds the paper high and reads with dramatic emphasis.

Sunil shakes his head. "Not here," he says, "It couldn't happen in an area like this. There may be trouble stirred up by some nationalist Hindus for a time but it can't last, after all India has a secular constitution and the majority of people don't want violence."

Night ceaselessly trembles her feet, providing the constant rustle and shimmer of ankle bells while Rupa stands on the roof looking at the wrong way round moon before going to bed. She remembers how, when her plane circled over Calcutta before making its final descent, the crescent moon had spiraled with them, reflected like a searchlight in the myriad waters of Bengal.

The family assume she shares their faith and she's said nothing to alter that, just as at home she says nothing about how meaningless she finds Sunday services. She always goes to Church because she knows Ma needs her to be there. As a child she avoided sermons by escaping to Sunday School where she enjoyed the songs and stories, but when the leaders prayed Rupa would blush in embarrassment. She couldn't bear to hear their devoted and adoring tones, the unconcealed emotion as they confessed and pleaded, and generally made fools of themselves before a make-believe God. She would giggle to cover the shame she felt on their behalf, until one of them suspended his performance, opening his eyes to glare and reprimand her for her levity. Even now Rupa remains an observer who only experiences the divine secondhand, as it is manifest in the humble or sentimental or sternly pious faces of the congregation.

Much more to Rupa's taste, when she was young, was the feel of the hard edges of her illustrated Bible with its shiny bright cover, through the compacted softness of her pillow. Lying on her back, head pressed firmly onto the flat book, she gained the strength needed to dispel those fearful nightly thoughts. Or the little silver cross which she hid amongst the pencil shavings and scraps of crumbling eraser in her pencil case, and peered at or touched before beginning an exam. These practical, straightforward expressions of religion she understood, they had the advantage of not involving a supernatural third party.

Where does she stand on the question of Nirmal babu's hypocrisy? On the whole she has to vote in his favor, at least on the general principle of having private opinions which you don't openly express, even when pressed. Rupa does that on many issues all the time, most people do don't they. Her father handled today's events with skill and composure, she respects him for that. As to what he actually believes in his heart, well that is a different matter. Religious beliefs come into a separate category because of the supernatural element, the conviction that you are obeying an external power, that's the dangerous part. Once you believe that then the welfare of your wife or husband, your children, friends, neighbors, all can be sacrificed, and the justification for this is easy, is the essence of your faith.

In the moonlight Rupa can just make out the shadowy shapes of broken marigold plants on either side of the gate, trampled by onlookers as they stood around waiting for something to happen.

CHAPTER EIGHT

The adults have gathered on the veranda; Nirmal babu is slumped in his easy chair, Rupa sits on the iron bed beside Chhaya who is picking over grains of rice spread out on a bamboo tray, Sunil sits on the veranda steps from where he can look out towards his birds, Jayanti has brought through a chair from the kitchen. Earlier Rupa mentioned to Sunil that she'd like to visit her mother's relatives, a simple request that she imagined could be quietly arranged in order to avoid distress to her father who would be certain to object. But what seems to her a clear straightforward proposal is being teased out and worried at, analyzed, dissected and pulled apart, until its edges are so frayed that its original form is beyond recognition. Rupa practises deep breathing and struggles to be patient. She's used to making her own decisions, and even, at work, to having some control over other people's lives. Now she feels quite powerless, but is shrewd enough to see that steady persistence will get her what she wants.

"How will they know that Rupa's going to visit? We'll have to tell them first, otherwise they might not be at home."

"She can't just turn up without warning."

"Rubbish! Someone's bound to be at home, no one leaves a house empty, someone or other will be guarding it."

"If you want to tell them first that means an extra journey, and supposing they aren't there when you go to tell them?"

"Anyway we're not absolutely sure who lives there now. Poltu mama used to work in the shop, and I guess he and his brothers kept it on when his father died, but we don't know that. Supposing they don't live there any longer?"

"Of course they still live there, such a big house with a shop attached, an established business. Why would they leave it? Where would they go?"

"Listen, listen to me. I don't like the idea at all. Why does she need to go there?" Nirmal babu's peevish question is ignored.

"Sunil will have to go on the way back from school and see what they say. Just sound them out about the idea."

"Maybe they won't want to see Rupa."

"What a stupid thing to say, of course they'll want to see her! Does any one not want to see their own relative, a close relative like Rupa?" This makes Rupa feel especially uncomfortable. The answer of course is yes, some people don't want to see their relatives.

"And how will she get there anyway? She can't travel alone."

"Does it mean Sunil will have to stay with her all the time?"

"Or I could take her there, come back here and go again to fetch her."

"Would they let him do that, or insist he stayed too?"

"She doesn't need to go. Why does she want to go?" Nirmal babu's voice is rising in volume and agitation.

"What do you think, can Rupa manage the trains?"

"It would be impossible for her when the trains are crowded, so she'd have to avoid office time."

"I think I'd be alright on the train, I've done it before. So long as someone is with me." Rupa judges it to be the right moment to speak for herself. At home she's trained herself not to interrupt, but would never be heard at all if she followed that rule now. Surely that can't be Ma sitting beside her, arms crossed, shoulders quivering with barely controlled mirth?

"So she'd have to come back early afternoon to miss the rush, and go late morning for the same reason."

"But she can't do that, it'll look as if she expects to eat with them."

91

"Is she going to eat there? Better to eat here and then go, don't you think?"

"At least drink tea with them, so they won't be offended."

"But they'll want to feed her, she must stay for a meal. Anything else would be very rude." It occurs to Rupa that Jayanti would love to accompany her, but can't because of her loyalty to … to what exactly? To her father, to the family's reputation?

"If Rupa goes this time, are they going to think we want to keep in touch in the future?"

"Are they going to want to see Priya and Bijoy?"

"How would our children feel about that?"

"What should she take for them? Will she just take shondesh?"

"She can't do that, she can't just take sweets! She'll have to give them something from England."

"Do you have any small presents left, Rupa?"

"But we don't know what ages the children are. Poltu mama had two sons, what, about my age, two or three years older maybe?"

"And daughters, younger than Jayanti I think."

"So their children could be any age, we just don't know."

"No one has answered me! You can't explain can you? Why does she need to go at all?" Nirmal babu is shouting now, getting up from his seat in exasperation.

"Don't worry Baba, you don't need to worry. Remember Rupa's come from a long way off, it's natural she wants to visit as many people as possible. I'll take care that it's all done properly. It won't affect the rest of us in any way." Sunil goes over to his father and places a calming hand on his back.

Chhaya has finished cleaning the rice and is ready to return to the kitchen. She pauses beside her father-in-law for a few moments, comforting him by her attentiveness, fetching him his cigarettes and a glass of water. She catches Sunil's eye and silently they agree that the discussion is over for now. Sunil goes out to tend his birds, and as he passes Rupa he screws up both eyes in a reassuring double wink accompanied by the slightest tilt of his head.

Rupa reflects that the process is similar to what happens on training days when course participants are asked to "unpack" a concept, or brainstorm round a new idea. All that's missing is a flip chart and some felt-tip pens. Amazingly, the whole thing has been conducted without a single reference to Ma, in spite of the fact that it's her relatives who are at the center of the discussion.

Rupa picks up the broken grains and tiny white stone chips that Chhaya dropped on the floor as she cleaned the rice, and tosses them one by one into the yard where the stupid hen, who has left her bowl half way up the stairs in search of food, pecks at them. Rupa waits for a while to see if Jayanti wants to say something, then at last follows Chhaya into the kitchen to help cut vegetables.

Jayanti stays where she is, brooding. All this fuss, this eagerness to satisfy Rupa's every whim, reminds her of the story of the prodigal son and his resentful older brother. Returning for a short holiday after an absence of several years, Rupa only has to express a desire to meet Ma's relatives and everyone falls over themselves in the attempt to organize a visit. Whereas Jayanti has lived here all her life, contributing to the household income and taking her share of responsibility for the children's upbringing, yet no one has ever offered to take her to Poltu mama's house. Did it never occur to Sunil, when they were still young, that Jayanti needed some contact with her female relatives? It was alright for Rupa, she had a mother to guide her through adolescence, but Jayanti, living as she did with a father and an older brother, had to learn second hand through friends about the mysteries of womanhood.

Goodness knows she can be outspoken and assertive when she needs to be, so why has she never insisted on getting in touch with Ma's family? The truth is Jayanti knows, has always known, that her father is terrified of losing her as he once lost his wife and youngest daughter. This fear also explains why she remains unmarried. There have been a few halfhearted attempts to find her a suitable partner, but everyone knows it will never happen. Nirmal babu couldn't bear to let her go.

Sunil and Rupa look out of the gap above the plastic sheet which is strung across the front of the ricksha and now clings coldly to their legs. Passengers flatten themselves against the walls of the station platform, shoppers shelter in the mouths of sweet shops, determined travelers hitch up saris and trouser legs and step over filthy puddles, holding briefcases above their heads, handkerchiefs tied protectively round their wrist watches. The ricksha jolts uncomfortably over the uneven road surface, cursed by those it splashes with dirty water when, too late, they jerk themselves away as it rolls by. At last Sunil tells it to stop on the main shopping street, and pays the fare.

He crosses the concrete block which bridges the open drain running along the edge of the street, and enters the dark interior of the jewelry shop. Rupa waits self-consciously outside. Customers sitting on the bench in front of the low counter turn and stare at her. People walking past glance at her with brief curiosity, something about her appearance tells them that she doesn't quite belong. She wonders what it is, her expression, body language, hairstyle? Then a boy comes out of the shop with Sunil and leads them both through a narrow passageway to a wide wooden door which wobbles on its hinges when he rattles the heavy padlock rings.

"Who is it?"

"Someone to see Poltu babu." And the boy is off back to the shop with a grin at Sunil and Rupa, evidently proud of the part he's played on this important occasion. The door is opened by a girl whose small face has a frizzy golden halo of unoiled hair, and whose frock has turned grayish brown from too much laundering. Sunil makes a joke, but the girl's face remains solemn and she doesn't respond. They leave their shoes under the stairs beside the jumbled pile already there, and the girl shows them into a room where two chairs have been placed against the wall, like thrones thinks Rupa suddenly, as if in preparation for royalty whose subjects are about to pay homage. The room is very clean, the shining floors are perfectly smooth underfoot, the covers on the large bed are stretched taut over bolsters and folded bedding. There's not much light in the room and it's unnaturally quiet. Perhaps the chairs are not thrones but seats on which to await trial and execution, Rupa knows these silly thoughts come because she's nervous. Sunil, undaunted, is on his feet again, padding over to the doorway.

"Poltu mama? Mamima? We've arrived!"

Poltu mama, tall and dark and dignified and freshly groomed from his bath, greets them. Then Mamima, her face creased with smiles and uttering exclamations of delight, and then gradually sons and daughters-in-law, and daughters and sons-in-law, and cousins and grandchildren accumulate until the room is full of giggling, inquisitive, marveling relatives and neighbors. Rupa loves it. She answers questions, tells stories, elaborates and exaggerates, jokes and sympathizes, drinks tea and eats coconut sweets, holds babies and looks at photographs. One after another children bring their new Puja outfits for her to admire ("I got five!," "That's nothing, I got eight and my cousin in Delhi is sending me one more"), and climbs onto the roof to inspect building work in progress, space for another son and his new wife to start their married life.

Rupa doesn't even notice Sunil's departure until it's time to wash before eating the midday meal. And Ma is everywhere, feet tucked under her on the bed with the women, thin towel over her shoulder as she helps the children bathe under the pump, crouching on a low stool in the kitchen grinding jeera and frying fish, and quietly with Mamima in the thakur-ghor for the midday puja. Ma as a young woman, supple, agile, more animated than Rupa has ever seen her.

After eating their rice everyone disperses to a comfortable resting place. One after another they settle down in rows on the beds or on floor mats, where conversations continue softly, accompanied by the rhythmic thump of infants being patted to sleep. Poltu mama was served his food first so he is already asleep, his snoring like the regular to and fro of a mechanical saw, the juddering as metal teeth bite into wood and then silence as it is pulled back for the next cut. Mamima lies beside Rupa and ruffles her hair, touches her cheek, lifts her hand to study the carefully tended nails.

"How's your mother?"

"She's well. She works in a job she really enjoys, and she's always busy doing things for the Church. We have some good friends. But ... she never tells me anything about this family, nor about when she was married. It may sound strange, but we never talk about those things at all." It's so easy to slip into this conversation, Rupa had worried it might be difficult to get started.

"I was married before your mother left home, so I knew her all the time she was with Nirmal. At first she used to bring Sunil and Jayanti here to see us and we were sometimes invited to their house. I remember we went once around Christmas time, but we didn't stay. It was awkward because they lived in school quarters, but we could have stayed if they'd wanted us to. Nirmal used to pretend Miss Featherstone would disapprove, we realized that was just an excuse. When Sunil was born Miss Featherstone herself invited my mother-in-law to stay at the school, and she stopped there for more than a month."

"What was my mother like then, when she was younger?" Rupa tries to sound casual but she is tense, hoping nothing will interrupt this precious moment. It feels as if she's opening an expensive bottle (perfume or champagne) she's wanted for a long while to buy, but is only now able to afford. She looks away, sensing that the intensity of her gaze is unnatural.

"What was she like? To begin with she was happy when she came here. We never let her help with any work, because she was the only daughter, she was special and we treated her like a queen. She'd go from room to room and talk to everyone, then when her father came back from the shop for his rice she'd sit by him and watch him eat, and ask him how the business was doing, perhaps look at some of his new designs for rings and bangles. After her own meal she'd lie beside her mother and they'd talk, hour after hour." Mamima rolls onto her back and crosses her ankles, spreads out her damp gray hair and reaches for a thin sheet with which she covers herself up to the shoulders. *Please don't go to sleep, please keep talking.*

"As soon as they arrived Sunil and Jayanti would go off to play with the other children, one of the women would see they bathed and ate their rice. While she was here she would forget her own children, as if she was hungry for her mother, just like

96

any married daughter I suppose. We understood, we weren't jealous, she never talked against us like some sisters-in-law do."

"When you went to her house how were things there, I mean, did she find it difficult having to manage the household all alone? Did my father realize how hard it was for her? She had no mother-in-law to show her how to do things." Rupa is interested in everything about Ma, but time is limited. She has to use all her skill now to bring the conversation round to what she wants to know, to extract the required information.

"She seemed to manage alright. In some ways it's easier not to have a mother-in-law in control of the household." Mamima chuckles softly as if at a forgotten memory, and Rupa is afraid she'll start talking about her own early experiences of marriage.

"I mean...."

Mamima lays a kind· hand on Rupa's arm. "Do you think I'm stupid? I know very well what you mean. You're wondering why your mother is in England and your father is here. You're wondering what could have made her go to live thousands of miles away, taking her baby but leaving her other two children behind. Then not keep in touch with them or with her own parents. You're wondering why her husband let her go, and you can't ask her because she won't talk about it, and nor would your father if you ever found the courage to ask him."

"I just thought perhaps you saw something which might help explain it, how they were together as husband and wife. Or if she told her mother things when she was visiting here, and later you heard what'd been said." Rupa is overwhelmed with gratitude that Mamima is making it so easy. She reaches out and begins to move her fingers up and down the pale smooth skin on the inside of Mamima's forearm, tapping her fingertips like light rain.

"As husband and wife? Nirmal was considerate, he seemed to understand what life was like for her, more thoughtful than most other men I'd say. He didn't expect her to be always in the house, of course she had to do her own cooking, but he encouraged her to sing and play the harmonium, go visiting and attend women's meetings. He was fairly serious, much older than her in his outlook, an old-fashioned husband, you know, treating her like a child who needs to be molded. Once or twice I saw him fly into a rage, not often, only if he was really upset.

"They were very different you see, she was bright and eager, restless and full of ideas, always making plans. We knew she wasn't happy, that she resented the way he treated her. She wasn't sullen or quarrelsome, that's not what I mean, nor did she complain behind his back, she just didn't respond to him in the way you'd expect. How to explain? They never laughed into each other's eyes, and you couldn't imagine them whispering together at night." Mamima giggles, recalling the whispered midnight secrets of her own marriage.

"And I think he found it difficult with us, with her family. He wasn't happy about her coming here too often, and when we went there he wasn't relaxed, he treated us well enough but it wasn't natural, as if he was making a big effort. He didn't want us near the children, that was the main thing with him, he thought we might influence them against being Christian. Once we gave Sunil and Jayanti clothes for Puja, and he insisted they were given back. I can remember how embarrassed and ashamed your mother was, and the way Jayanti screamed and sulked to keep her new frocks. It wasn't that Nirmal minded us giving them clothes, it was because they were for Puja, as if that contaminated them somehow."

"As if Ma had to choose between her husband and her parents?" It isn't really a question, more a musing born of Rupa's observation of so many marriages, of so many situations. Always either this or that, who do you love most, which comes first – husband or children, wife or mother, job or family.

"A Bengali girl doesn't choose, when she's married she only goes to her father's house if her husband lets her. At least that used to be the case then, things are different now, these days most wives do whatever they like regardless of in-laws and husbands," Mamima sighs.

"On the whole I think English couples tend to stick closer to the wife's family, mothers and daughters against the rest. Women involve their own mothers in their married lives, their homes and children. Men don't like it, hence all those mother-in-law jokes."

"Anyway, your mother came here less and less often, and when she did come she would be alone and sad. He stopped inviting us altogether, and then...." Mamima raises her eyebrows meaningfully, lifts a hand and twists her wrist in the air, signifying "that's all." But Rupa doesn't know then what, so she prompts,

"Then?"

"Then apparently she disappeared altogether, and Nirmal came here one day in a terrible state demanding we hand her over to him and threatening to call the police. He wouldn't come inside just stood by the main door and shouted. We didn't know where she was, so your Poltu mama went out and reasoned with him for ages, and eventually poor Nirmal went away sobbing. A crowd of neighbors gathered and wanted to know what was happening, people went on gossiping about it for weeks."

There is a silence during which Rupa sees her father's tear-soaked face, not an old man's face but an imaginary younger version, and watches his despairing footsteps as he stumbles back alone down the narrow lane. Mamima sits up stiffly, struggles off the bed, rearranges her sari and, calling to her husband, goes to see about making his afternoon tea. But she hasn't told Rupa what Nirmal had said, or why Ma had disappeared.

Later Poltu mama, dressed and ready to return to the shop for the afternoon session, comes back into the room. Rupa takes the dust of his feet and he wishes her well. Mamima asks him, "Aren't you going to send a message for Rupa's mother, for your sister?" He looks sternly at Rupa, "Would she want me to?" and walks proudly out of the room.

Poltu mama's eldest grandson is to accompany Rupa on her journey home, and on the way he'll show her some of the best Kali Puja pandals. The matter was settled before Rupa arrived, and she's not sure that it has received Sunil's approval. However she's not complaining, for he is the guide and escort she would certainly have chosen had she been consulted. She noticed him at the pump while she was eating. He was bathing with only a gamchha knotted round his waist ("loins" that's a better word), the wet cloth clinging to his buttocks and to the front of his thighs. As she brought her rice-filled fingers up to her mouth her eyes covered his body, watching the muscles bunch and stretch under the moist skin as he bent forward to work the pump and then reached up to pour water over himself. She noted the shifting shadows under each shoulder blade, and when he undid the gamchha in the process of putting on his lungi, she glimpsed the perfect little dark hollows at each side of the base of his spine. He had his back towards her so she couldn't see his face, only the occasional hint of thick eyelashes, overhanging bottom lip, and the fine line of his moustache.

When he turned his head and met her eyes she continued to look, and his playful grin told her he had inherited the same enjoyment of life that Priya possesses. But Priya's sense of fun is naïve and innocent, at least for the present, whereas Rupa feels sure this young man's is not.

When it's time to leave, Rupa lets them comb her hair and arrange it in whatever style they choose, cream her face with Snow, dust her neck with powder, and outline her eyes with kajol. There is competition over who will carry out this adornment, and she surrenders to the skilful hands of the victor, a daughter of the house about Rupa's own age who deals robustly with interference from the eager jostling group which looks on. Rupa hopes that the results achieved will make her young escort proud to be with her, she doesn't want to let him down. As they walk together they might encounter some of his friends, at least be seen by neighbors. Finally a bindi is chosen and stuck onto her forehead, then, freeing herself from the fondly clutching hands and still surrounded by tearful farewell smiles, she goes away down the narrow lane.

He is self-conscious and walks a little ahead, turning awkwardly to answer her questions. She is his pishima, a different generation, and she can feel this barrier restraining his behavior and the content of his conversation. She'd hoped he would tell her about the current social scene, girlfriends – what couples do and where; drugs – which kinds and who uses them; alcohol – as for drugs; gay relationships – attitude of peers. Impossible! Okay, so let's concentrate on Kali Puja pandals.

They pass a small local specimen, a simple single-peaked affair the main body of which is covered in purple cloth. The sloping roofs of the four storeys, which decrease in width as the structure narrows to a high tower, and the mock pillars along the lowest section, are colored white, and white figures and patterns decorate the upper layers. Leaving Rupa standing a little way off, he pauses for a few moments to chat to the group of young men who sit on a bench near the wooden steps leading up to the doorway. He comes back to her shaking his head, Kali has not yet been installed. As they reach the busiest part of the town they see more pandals. One magnificent green and yellow edifice rises high above them, topped by three domed turrets, an elaborate garden of pot plants laid out round the entrance. Another, cool and refined in sea blue and white, has a double arched porch, steps covered in blue cloth, and a little balcony on the second storey. Groups gather in crooked-neck admiration before moving on to view the next one. Loudly distorted film songs agitate the air and the streets here are crowded, which makes conversation difficult but Rupa tries anyway.

"Are you learning the jewelry trade from your father or do you have other plans?"

"I don't fancy sitting in front of a fire all day melting and shaping gold, much too hot. Anyway I have no talent for design, or so they tell me. My younger brother's good at that, fortunately he's keen on the business side too. Me, I'm in the first year of a B.Sc. We'll see, who knows what'll happen!" He grins widely, obviously he's not dedicated to following a carefully planned career.

"Do they let you decide for yourself, I mean is there any pressure for you to take over the shop eventually? Poltu mama, your grandfather that is, followed his father, and then your father is following him. It's been handed down through the eldest son, so I wondered whether they expected you to continue the tradition." There's a niche here, a chance to find out about inter-generational tensions, but he laughs off her suggestion.

"Not with us, no, nothing like that. There weren't the opportunities then perhaps. I don't know, but my family's happy for me to go on studying and then find whatever job I can. I know people, have contacts in a few companies. Something will turn up."

He directs her attention towards a ricksha van which waits beside the road. On it stands a life size image of Kali, her blue body naked except for a decoration round the waist which obscures her unseemly bits. The palms of her four hands are painted bright red. Round her neck hangs a long string of yellow and pink male heads, their eyes peacefully shut, and thick locks of black hair coil to her knees. Sheets of newspaper are tied over her face using a strand of her own hair for string, her large mixing bowl breasts are completely exposed but her face is concealed. A young boy sits cross-legged on the van holding Kali's legs to steady her, he gazes upwards at the hidden face not at the breasts. Rupa is inexplicably convinced that the face behind the newspaper screen is Ma's face, sad and pensive. Her escort explains that the image is being taken to one of the pandals, and that the newspaper will remain in place until the goddess is installed.

They climb the steps of the next pandal and gaze with others at the image which is arrayed in gorgeous red and gold. Her blue face is serene, her eyes steady and calm under beautifully arched brows. But Rupa knows that this is only the mask that the goddess assumes when the newspaper is removed. Suddenly she no longer wants to know about the state of the family in Bengal today, she is only interested in what her nephew has heard about Ma.

"Your family is close then, I mean you all look after one another." He tilts his head in agreement and a puzzled fold appears between his brows. "But what about my mother, your grandfather's sister? Doesn't anyone talk about her? Why did they let her go away without trying to stop her, and then not try to find where she'd gone?" This isn't fair and she knows it. He is her guide and escort, her nephew, and does not belong to her search. He has no speaking part in this episode. They are both silent for a while as they stand and look at Kali, radiant beneath the glass chandeliers, her husband lying prone and pathetic at her feet.

"I have heard them talking about her, of course I have." This is very brave of him, he's responding to Rupa's need and ignoring the conventions. "I've always known Dadu's sister is in England

and that we don't have anything to do with her husband and his family, even though they still live here." She won't ask anything further, it's his choice, but if he does keep talking she will listen.

"The impression I got was that her husband was proud, thought a lot of himself, and didn't like our family much." Rupa nods, this confirms Mamima's account. "But I don't think they blamed him for her running away, not directly at least. There was something else." He glances at Rupa's face, his eyes still show the same gaiety but now he's weighing up whether to proceed, whether she can take the next bit, indeed whether he can voice the words. Her breathing is shallow and she doesn't look at him as she waits. Cold fingers tangle her entrails and she is weakened by nausea.

"Some scandal involving a young man. Maybe he was a teacher at the school, at least he used to go to the house to teach her, I'm sure I've heard them say that. I can't tell you what happened exactly but I know it was bad enough for her own father to feel he couldn't take her back to live with them." She wants to laugh, this is so unexpected and absurd! She mustn't give the impression that she doubts his words, that would be ungrateful considering the courage he's shown, but it's impossible for her to reply without doing so.

So she smiles at him to let him know she's okay, and suggests they continue towards the station. He is eager to show her a small pandal in the area behind the station where Kali is portrayed differently, as Kali of the funeral pyres, the goddess who inhabits the burning places of the dead. The figures here make up a tableau. The dark blue goddess runs unclothed across the platform. With one of her hands she holds up a male figure wearing a tiger skin, grasping him by a handful of his hair. He has a wound in his neck from which red wires of blood spurt. At the front of the platform a large black head whose eyes and brows are thickly drawn in red, and on whose forehead is a third eye, catches the blood on its protruding tongue. The expression on Kali's face as she holds up her victim is one of wild triumphant rage, a powerful woman not to be crossed. Rupa is drawn to this portrayal, full of anger and strength, preferring it to the sweet serenity of the more popular images.

She remains absorbed in the tableau until he urges her to come away so they can catch the train before it gets impossibly busy. Circles of drummers crouch outside the station, broadcasting their skills and hoping to be hired by one of the pandal organizers or a wealthy family, to play for the evening puja. When the two of them reach the platform, passengers are already standing shoulder to shoulder.

All night drums beat, fireworks explode, conch shells hoot, tongues ululate, and films songs are cranked up to an incredible volume then blasted forth through mikes. As she lies cocooned inside the soft fibres of the mosquito net Rupa's thoughts emerge from the paralysis that has held them on the journey home in the train, body wedged against body crushing special puja clothes, and then by ricksha to the house. Instead of dismissing the ricksha, her nephew asked it to wait while he delivered her safely into Sunil's care, and then he left without even setting foot on the veranda steps. All according to Poltu mama's instructions no doubt. She coped well with the questions which attacked her as soon as he'd gone, painting what she hoped was an authentic and happy picture of her visit to Poltu mama's house but without providing too much detail.

Now her blood is beginning to flow again. So, she has to admit that in theory it's quite possible Ma had a lover. Rupa has never thought of that but you don't, do you? Not your own mother, not without some evidence to start you thinking. Now she has her nephew's remarks to consider, nothing very definite but certainly evidence to be taken seriously. This thought in itself is difficult to comprehend, but the part that has really shaken her is the timing of it all. Rupa was only two or three months old when Ma left India, if there had been an affair, then could the unknown young man, one of the teachers perhaps, be her real father? It could explain why she has no warmth for Nirmal babu but does feel a bond with everyone else. A matter of blood.

While part of Rupa's mind continues to puzzle over dates and genetics, somewhere else desolation begins to spread, filling the spaces inside her until she is forced to stop and allow herself to focus on it. Just as Nirmal babu is starting to emerge as a complete person, his kinship to her is thrown into question. Rupa is surprised to find she grieves for him and resents the intrusion of another player. She wonders to whom she actually owes allegiance, to the only man she has known as father, or to this new shadowy figure who might be her biological parent. Her imagination resumes its activity and, despite pangs of guilt, she can't help wondering what he was like, this man whom Ma loved enough to risk everything. With the shyness of the newly acquainted, Rupa tries to conjure up the outlines of this romantic possibility. Her slight stature, straight and wilful hair, along with other facets of her appearance which can't be traced to Ma, these could be inherited from this other man. Some of her mannerisms and personality traits likewise. For a while she's lost in a mist of imagining, partly pleasurable, though uncertainty makes the process painful too.

Later Rupa's natural curiosity prompts her to consider the messy questions; who did the chasing, was Ma easily persuaded, was the relationship with Nirmal babu already foundering, was it mainly a physical thing (ten years into marriage, sex could have grown stale), what about the practicalities – for instance where did Ma leave the children while it was going on? How did Nirmal find out, what did he say and do?

That question arrests the progress of her thoughts, the scene is too pitiable to contemplate. She draws up her knees, tries to choke the tears, then lets them flow stinging hot onto scrunched up handfuls of bedsheet pressed against her eyes. She doesn't know why she's crying; for Nirmal as he discovers he's been betrayed by the wife whom he adores, or for Ma in her desperation. Perhaps she weeps also for herself, a young woman unable to claim independence because she can't escape the bonds of loving entanglement with her mother.

Rupa has had boyfriends, some of whom developed into lovers, but when it comes to the point of announcing a break, a new life separate from Ma's, she can't do it. The vacuum of her mother's past leaves Rupa wholly responsible, burdened. In the absence of Ma's history, Rupa's future is frozen. She knows she has to fill that vacuum, however distressing or disturbing the detail. This then is the reason she wants to find out about her parents' marriage, nothing to do with Life Story Books, the explanation she offered Jayanti on that first evening. No, she needs to know about the past because she believes that knowledge will free her from the life threatening weight she carries.

Admitting this to herself brings on a fresh burst of crying. Her shoulders jerk with each gasping sob as spasms of self-pity pass through her. Rupa covers her mouth with the tear-soaked bedsheet to stifle the sound of her moaning.

CHAPTER NINE
1971
~♥~

At first Mary didn't recognize her. The woman's face was hidden by the sari pulled forward right over her head, and instead of the usual carefree manner of her walking, this figure approached rapidly, keeping in the shadows close to the wall like an escaping fugitive, with frequent backward glances. Mary hadn't recognized the voice either, the strained little call which halted her striding progress towards her room. She was anticipating the after-school cups of tea, and the small squares of rubbery toast on which she would spread butter from a neat cardboard packet (she had recently acquired a fridge which made life so much easier), and homemade guava jam so solid that it threatened to bend the teaspoon. A strained little call, nothing like the strong happy voice of the woman who read the lesson in Church and sang Crusader choruses with the children. It was the sight of the baby held tightly against the woman's side and half covered by her sari, which at last cleared the puzzlement from Mary's brow. The sleeping baby's head fitted into the crook of its mother's elbow while her hand supported its lower body.

"You alright? Baby sick?" The woman had caught up with her now and as Mary stretched her hand to lift aside the cloth hanging over the baby's face, she could feel the sweating heat from its mother's body and hear her panting. Fear? Of what? Was that bruising round her eyes or just dark patches caused by lack of sleep, you couldn't always tell with their complexions. The woman was clutching the baby too tightly, perhaps she was protecting it from someone. Whatever it was that had happened, Mary wondered why Nirmal's wife had come to her instead of seeking out her own husband.

"Where Nirmal?"

"He's busy giving tuition. I don't want him to know where I am." She shook her head frantically, looked behind her once more, and gestured urgently towards the door of Mary's room. The same unfamiliar voice, tight and tense.

Mary felt in the pocket of her cotton frock and drew out first a handkerchief, lace-edged and still neatly folded, then three keys attached to a ring. She selected one and used it to undo the lock. The distraught figure squeezed past her as the door opened, and then moved to a position against one wall, first checking that she couldn't be seen through either of the windows. Usually the door remained open when Mary was at home, but she knew that now she must close it, that in fact Nirmal's wife would have preferred it to be locked again. Her desperation communicated itself to the room, furniture edged forward ready to respond to this emergency, eager to provide the setting in which the drama would unfold. Mary registered the changed atmosphere and felt herself step, with some relish as well as trepidation, into crisis management mode. First she needed a full explanation, she must have that before she could plan her intervention.

"Sit now, I make tea. You put baby here on trunk." Mary busied herself arranging two cushions on top of the large trunk, leaving just enough space between them to create a safe haven for the load which Nirmal's wife still pressed against her body. After checking that the spot was not visible from outside, the mother placed her baby between the cushions and crouched beside it, resting one of her hands lightly on its chest. The baby's eyes were screwed up shut, two lines deeply engraved in the notch at the top of its nose between the eyes. Nirmal's wife shook her head rapidly so that her sari slipped back and lay in folds round her shoulders, then she struck her forehead repeatedly with the open palm of her free hand. No, thought Mary, a cup of tea isn't needed right now, I have to relieve some of this tension first. She knelt down beside the crouching woman and attempted to lay a reassuring hand on her back, but as she did so Nirmal's wife turned abruptly towards her so that Mary's hand was dislodged and dropped limply by her side.

"Miss Featherstone, forgive me for coming to you like this. I didn't know what else to do, my situation is quite desperate. I have to get away, right now from my husband, and I have to take my baby with me. Something has happened and I can't tell you what, but it is so serious that he will not have me in the house again. Nor can I go back to my father's house. Please be kind to me and find somewhere for me to stay, me and my baby, some place where my husband won't be able to follow." Although she was clearly exhausted and distressed she spoke steadily and looked straight at Mary as she made her request. Hearing its mother's voice, the baby opened its unfocused eyes, moved its head irrationally from side to side, and waved its frail fists aimlessly in the air.

"Slow, slow! You tell what happen, why Nirmal angry, what make him angry, where Sunil and Jayanti, why you no go home. First you tell, then I help. Understand?" Mary shuffled over to a cane stool and raised herself onto it. "Nirmal teach in my school. I ask him also what wrong. You talk, he talk, and everything good again." How frustrating this inability of hers to gain a proper command of Bengali, it meant delicate interactions were impossible. Mary didn't blame Nirmal's wife for the look of disappointment, for the disdain with which she regarded the English lady. What mattered now was how things were said, choice of words, connotations, subtle meanings, as much as what was said. And she couldn't do it, so she compensated with tone of voice, facial expression, exaggerated gestures, banal interjections.

Nirmal's wife watched and listened silently as Mary struggled to explain that everyone's opinion must be taken into consideration, that although she was very upset at the moment maybe she would feel differently after a rest, that nothing could be done in a hurry because the whole family would be affected, and that she had serious responsibilities as a Christian wife and mother. She listened with patience but offered no responses to ease the tortured delivery which lurched and lunged but never reached its target. Eventually Mary fell silent while Nirmal's wife continued to stare unforgivingly at her. The baby moved its head restlessly this way and that and little whimpers came from its puckered mouth.

"Miss Featherstone, it was you who planned our marriage, you arranged for my baptism, you took me from my father's house and brought me to this school, now you have to find somewhere for me to hide. You can't deny me help because you, you personally, brought about this situation in which I find myself. I'm telling you I need to live somewhere away from my husband. I realize this will take time to organize so for now I must go into shelter, into a place you will find for me and my baby." The words were spoken with dignity, without hesitation.

Damn the language! Because of it one might almost think that this young woman, the wife of a teacher in Mary's school, was in control of the situation, an illusion which was derived entirely from the medium of their communication. The facts were quite otherwise of course. Nevertheless with her last words Nirmal's wife had played the trump card, held a pistol to Mary's head, found her Achilles heel, whatever clichéd metaphor you chose to adopt, and it rather seemed that Mary would have to comply, at least temporarily.

"My husband will return from tuition in less than an hour. Before then I must take my baby somewhere safe." She knew she had won, the composure with which she made this clear demand contrasted so completely with Mary's stumbling. She gathered up the crying baby and soothed it with soft meaningless sounds, then informed Mary that she was going into the bedroom to feed her baby in privacy, and that this would take roughly twenty minutes, implying that when she emerged again she expected to be taken to a place of concealment. Mary stood up and blocked her path.

"You know enough English to understand when I say that I refuse to be pressurized in this way! Listen, you must realize I can't act so quickly without consulting Nirmal first. He would accuse me of being on your side against him, and I still don't have any idea of what's going on, what's happened between you." Despite the authority of Mary's manner the gaps between and round the words were filled with uncertainty. "You always seemed happy enough, can't you tell me what went wrong?" Ignoring this intervention Nirmal's wife moved towards the bedroom, so that unless she'd been prepared to engage in physical restraint Mary had to stand aside.

As the bedroom door closed Mary collapsed onto the trunk, causing the lid to creak as it sagged under her weight. She didn't need this. There were enough problems at school in connection with the court case which some parents, supported it had to be admitted by a few of the teachers, had filed against the headmaster. Selected in a hurry and without sufficient prayer after George Koshy's sudden departure for more lucrative employment in the Middle East, his successor had proved to be a disastrous choice. Probably as a reaction against George's lack of humor, Mary and the Bishop had fallen for a jovial character who during his interview outlined grand ideas for developing the school, but who in practice had spent most of his time hobnobbing with the township's wealthier families. Of course this soon lead to favoritism towards certain pupils, and thence to factions and politicking amongst guardians and in the staff room. And eventually to a court case.

Now the headmaster actually spent more time with his lawyer planning his defence than he did managing the school, which meant that Mary hadn't been able to leave as planned, to take up a less demanding position in a retreat house. A lovely old building with huge doors, cool ceilings you would need a ladder to reach, full length broad verandas, echoing bathrooms and a curving flight of wide stairs on which ghosts of the Raj trod ceaselessly. Instead she was still tied up in this concrete industrial township with its little box quarters and little status-conscious officials.

Actually Mary was relieved in some ways that Mr. Koshy wasn't around to witness this rift between Nirmal and his wife, it would have been so humiliating to see the self-righteous "I told you so" look on his face. He had never been happy with her plan, her acted prophecy, her attempt to bring commitment and a sense of responsibility into the lives of the school staff. Then she remembered James Lawson. She had discussed the plan with him

111

in its earliest stages and he too had counseled caution. He was back in London now as one of the Society's area secretaries. Hopefully Nirmal would sort out whatever was wrong, and James need never hear of this at all. Why hopefully? Of course Nirmal would be able to talk his wife round, she had a genuinely good heart, a real love for her husband and children, and for the Lord. And she had his youngest child with her. But in the meantime Mary must take her somewhere to cool down, otherwise she just might do something stupid. You could never be sure, they seemed in control from the outside but could suddenly do terrible things to themselves, railway lines, kitchen fires ... no she couldn't take any chances, must arrange something immediately.

And while she deliberated and planned, rising to the occasion, testing her resourcefulness, meeting the challenge, wisps of smoke began to seep into the space which contained her thoughts, an irritating choking smoke which gradually became denser until she could no longer ignore it. Had she been wrong all along, had she manipulated lives to meet not God's will but her own wilful desires, and were the terrible consequences beginning to unfold?

A light blue car stuttered up the drive and stammered to a halt beside the circular flower bed cut from a large secluded stretch of grass, and filled with evenly spaced, color co-ordinated plants. The steps which led up to the front door of the only A type quarter, the General Manager's bungalow, were lined on both sides with rows of pots. Clay pots fluted and crimped round the top like pie-crusts or jam tarts. Mrs. General Manager loved plants and enjoyed caring for them, but because of her elevated status could not be seen to work in the garden. Pot plants, however, were another matter, so she had assembled this collection which she herself tended, while she gave instructions to the mali concerning the garden. Varieties of hibiscus – one floating pink and frilly like a ballerina's fussy dress; another single scarlet flower, with long stamen golden barbed and tipped with five velvet globules, the goddess Kali's favorite, perfect in its simplicity; and rarer delicate white blooms with veins and centers stained deep purple. Also heavy-scented gardenias, white, ivory, and cream as the flowers slowly aged, and many small shrubs grown for the variegated hue and pattern of their leaves.

Mary turned to say a few words to the shrouded figure in the back seat, then climbed out of the car and ascended the steps. A young woman came to the shadowed doorway, and after a brief conversation opened the grills and ushered Mary inside.

It had occurred to Mary that to go straight to the top would be a brilliant move, a way of pre-empting future scandal. No one could later challenge her actions in the matter if mother and baby had found their first refuge in the GM's own home. Nirmal's wife had eventually agreed to come because she knew that Nirmal would never dream of searching for her here, now it was up to Mary to present the situation in such a way that the GM too agreed to her proposal.

A tall pale figure came noiselessly into the tastefully furnished room where Mary sat waiting, explained that her husband had not yet returned from his office and offered her visitor a choice of sherbet or tea, or perhaps something stronger if it wasn't too early in the day. Mrs. GM had just risen from her afternoon sleep, she looked elegantly weary, bored with her uneventful life, or perhaps bored with hearing about but being excluded from her husband's eventful life. She treated Mary with great courtesy but did not smile. Well this would test Mary's skills, thank goodness the woman spoke good English. Mary asked for sherbet and wondered whether she might bring in her companion who was still sitting outside in the car? Certainly, why didn't she say so earlier. While the cool drinks were being prepared and served with a selection of peeled and sliced fresh fruits, Mary brought mother and baby inside.

And then Mary maneuvered the conversation with practiced skill, using the baby to gain sympathy, allaying fears by stressing that the measure was only a temporary one, placing herself with Mrs. GM in the category of experience in contrast to the youth and immaturity of Nirmal's wife, suggesting that members of the Lions Club (of which Mrs. GM was currently president) would warmly approve of her generosity in helping this unfortunate woman.

113

So that when Mary finally left to drive her little car unsteadily back down the drive, Mrs. GM was cherishing the baby against her bosom, swaying her upper body from side to side while humming a lullaby remembered from her childhood, pausing only to give orders to her servant concerning the preparation of a room for mother and baby, and looking more alive than she had done since her own sons had gone away to jobs in Boston and Bombay.

Mary would have to walk past Nirmal's quarters on her way from the garage where she had left the car, back towards her own room. It was almost dark, by now he must have returned from his tuition, discovered his wife was missing and probably begun searching for her. Her stomach melted and her ears buzzed – how absurd! Who was Nirmal Sarkar that she should shrink from encountering him? Head up, shoulders back, big smile, hum a cheerful chorus, that's more like it.

As she reached his doorway from which elongated triangles of light projected onto the concrete passageway, she glanced behind the colorful curtain hanging there. Jayanti cross-legged on the bed was busy nursing the doll cradled in her lap, her brother beside her leant forward over the sheet of paper on which he was painting, near him he'd placed a cup of water for cleaning his brush between colors. No signs of distress there. Should she disturb them and ask to speak to their father? It might be best to confront Nirmal straightaway. As far as Mary knew no one had seen Nirmal's wife come to her room, or go off with her in the car, but you could never be sure, and anyway she wasn't planning to deceive Nirmal, just to insist that he allow his wife some time until she saw matters clearly again.

"Are you looking for me, Miss Featherstone?" He was only a few steps away and she hadn't noticed. He appeared to be in control, waiting respectfully for her reply, no tearing of hair or gnashing of teeth. Perhaps unnaturally controlled, a cold composure untypical of him.

"Nirmal! I didn't hear you coming. I was passing and noticed the children, how contented they looked. Have they eaten yet?"

Brightly, as if nothing had happened, let him be the first to mention his wife's absence. Nirmal drew the curtain to one side. Jayanti looked up and smiled at him, holding up her doll for his approval but saying nothing because Mary's presence made her shy. Nirmal nodded back at her. Sunil unconcerned continued to move his paintbrush over the paper, holding the sheet still with the fingertips of his other hand.

"They'll have their food in a little while. Why do you ask?" Nirmal let the curtain fall into place again sealing the children back inside the light of their home, and turned towards Mary who stood in the dusk outside. His voice was defensive and hard. "As I'm sure you've heard, my wife is not here. I told her this morning I didn't want her to stay in my house any longer. Perhaps you know where she is, but I'm not interested. I'm quite capable of taking care of my own son and daughter."

"I didn't mean to suggest you weren't! I was just making conversation. Yes, I know you and your wife have had some disagreement, I know she's gone off for a while. But when you say you're not interested in finding out where she is, then I don't believe you. Nirmal, you know very well you love her too much, far too much, for that to be true. And remember, she's taken your youngest daughter with her."

It was all going wrong, Mary had expected him to beg her to reveal his wife's hiding place, instead of which it was Mary who was encouraging him to ask. Why had his wife been afraid, thinking that he'd try to follow her? Who was putting on an act and who was being deceived? Mary found it hard to judge, as Nirmal spoke he looked past her not at her, she couldn't see his face clearly in the half light.

"Of course you always know best, Miss Featherstone, but I'm telling you I won't let her in this house ever again. She's made her choice, she knew what she was doing." Mary would rather he had wept and raged than adopt this polite reserve, cruelly concealing his fury from her. What did he mean, "she's made her choice?" This was pride, choosing not to share his anger or hurt with her, and she in turn was insulted, humiliated, to be excluded. She had almost counted him a loyal friend.

"Come on Nirmal, please trust me. Tell me what happened, surely you can tell me, and then I can persuade her to come back, to sort things out with you. For the children's sake. The children need their mother to be at home with them." A hint of command in her voice, the suggestion of authority, his headmistress speaking.

"You're not listening! I said I don't want her back!" His voice rose a few tones, jagged, fraying. Was he about to snap? But now his speech smoothed out and resumed its former neutral shade. "Excuse me while I go inside to give Jayanti and Sunil their food, and help them with their studies. You'll forgive me if I don't attend evening prayers today."

And that's pretty much how it continued. Mary gave him every opportunity over the next few days to admit he wanted to speak to his wife, even hinting that she could arrange this, but Nirmal concentrated stubbornly on his teaching responsibilities. The situation was much the same with his wife. When Mary made her daily visit to the bungalow, the woman repeated her demand that she be found somewhere safe to live, away from her husband. Mrs. General Manager grew steadily more devoted to the baby and protective of its mother, it was obvious the longer they were left in her house the more difficult it would be to persuade her to release them. Only when Mary reported news of Sunil and Jayanti did their mother cover her face to choke off dry little sobs, but she would not share her sorrow.

At first Mary couldn't identify the symptoms all this produced in her, although she knew they were distantly familiar. The ache in her throat, the shrinking of her thoughts under the livid bruise which swelled and throbbed inside her skull, the fierce need to be touched and embraced. At last she recognized them as the same feelings of rejection which permeated her childhood. She understood now that her parents should never have had children, they were far too much in love to make space for any offspring. Mary and her sister were kept on the outskirts of their parents' passionate relationship, rows and reconciliations. The beautiful bouquets gracefully accepted only to be tossed out of the kitchen window, the barely coded messages of lust with which the couple humiliated their daughters in public, the bedroom door locked

116

against loud knocks and kicking. Then, she did everything possible to break in. She remembered how she would jump back into the bathwater after her mother had carefully dried her and dressed her in a nightie, so that when her father came home he would have to turn his first attention to her, to scold her for her mischief. How she would deliberately spill and slop and mess at mealtimes, anything to disrupt her parents' tunnel intimacy.

This time Mary was outside the window peering through the smudged glass not at her parents' fire but at the formless feuding of Nirmal and his wife. The situation was ridiculous and couldn't be allowed to drag on for long, but what was she to do? If they refused to let her in to help work out a solution, then let them jolly well accept the consequences. (Why did the word "punish" creep up on her? That was unreasonable and unchristian.) The daughter of a Hindu family, now the mistreated wife of a Christian household, could so easily become the nucleus for scandal, for diplomatic reasons she must be removed far from the scene. Finance would present a problem. According to Nirmal's wife her father would accept no responsibility, and after eleven years of marriage, three children, and with a Hindu attitude to such matters, it was highly unlikely she'd even begin to consider another husband. Nor did she have the qualifications to secure a job where she could earn enough to keep herself and her child.

Then all at once Mary knew exactly what she was going to do, and as ever it came as a gift from God. Just a few weeks ago she had received a letter from a close friend, a retired missionary colleague, who wrote of severe arthritis and worrying signs of heart disease. In view of her deteriorating health this friend was looking for a live-in companion, but so far, in spite of a wide circle of Church contacts, she had drawn a blank. Of course Nirmal's wife was not an ideal candidate, her spoken English was poor and she had a small baby to care for, but these obstacles could be overcome, the baby might even bring joy into a life so afflicted with pain. Mary felt sure that when she described the circumstances, her friend would be only too keen to help. The timing was superb, and obviously meant. Mary would have to confess her part in the whole affair, but she didn't really mind that. She wasn't proud, just a trifle touchy, and could readily admit she sometimes got things wrong, or at least that her inspired plans didn't always turn out as she (or God) intended.

Unlike her contemporaries at missionary college, and later in the field, Mary didn't try to rein in or disguise her exuberance, her endless enthusiasm, or her emotions. Always ready to open her heart, rejoice or weep with those around her, acknowledge her weaknesses, and follow her latest vision to its fulfillment. Others were embarrassed by what they saw as her naïvety ("unpredictable," "sentimental," "impetuous" were adjectives she'd overheard), and avoided her because of it. They weighed up their options carefully, practised tact and caution, and relied on the considerable experience of their superiors. But Mary expected great things, wanted to achieve great things, now, not after years of patient waiting! It was the same when she was a schoolgirl. Her classmates merely moaned and whinged about being set too much homework, or being forced to miss morning break in order to finish their arithmetic, but she took immediate action. Once she tipped their teacher the Black Spot (she had just read *Treasure Island*), and led the whole class out into the playground on strike.

Yes, to send Nirmal's wife to England was a drastic move, Mary understood that well, but the situation was serious and demanded a drastic response. You had to be decisive, not wait around expecting matters to put themselves right. Mary would put the suggestion to her with a strong recommendation that she accept, and then telegram her English friend outlining her proposal. She could follow this up with a phone call from Calcutta, when she would explain the situation more fully. Once she adjusted to an English way of life, with her kind and capable nature Nirmal's wife would be a great comfort to Mary's friend, and would in turn be well-provided for. More permanent future plans, negotiations with immigration officials, could be made when Mary went on furlough next year.

"Would you like to come into the office, Miss Featherstone, rather than sit with them? It's getting crowded out here, you'd be more comfortable inside." The British Consul official curled his lip imperceptibly as he regarded the mass of people who had gathered in the Visa Department waiting room, inviting Mary with a sweep of his hand to join him and the other English personnel in their cool and orderly office. She smiled gratefully and began to stand up, but then glanced down at the diminutive figure beside her own tall frame, changed her mind and resumed her seat.

"That's very kind of you, but we'll just stay where we are. The baby might disturb you if we took it inside, don't worry about us. A glass of boiled water would be appreciated though, it's airless in here, stifling." The official again regarded the numerous bodies spread round the seats and walls and floor, and the widening of his nostrils said "not only hot but smelly." He brought a drink of chilled water which he handed to Mary, and then when Mary requested it, another for her companion in a thick roughly cut glass. They had waited over an hour already. Nirmal's wife was exhausted by the weight of the baby she carried, and the strain of encountering strange places and strange people, but she sat expressionless and resolute. Only a careful observer would notice the rapid rise and fall of her shoulders and the perspiration on her upper lip and forehead. She had knowingly put her future in Miss Featherstone's hands and was determined to hang on tight, for her baby's sake, to tread whatever path the English lady chose. Meanwhile Mary laughed with the children playing round their mothers' saris, joked with the weary women in an effort to cheer them, and reassured anxious fathers who consulted her about which forms and documents would be needed.

They had already spent two weeks in Calcutta, each day passed in visits to offices; BOAC for tickets that couldn't be issued without Passport and Entry Certificate and Tax Clearance, the Reserve Bank which couldn't issue Tax Clearance without letters of sponsorship from the country of destination signed by public notaries, the Passport Office where they stood two hours in a queue to reach a counter only to be told that they must come back the next day, the British Consul where they discovered that Entry Certificates depended amongst other things on production of return tickets, a medical center where they were offered a choice between actually having the obligatory vaccinations or obtaining the relevant stamps on payment of a small fee.

They traveled by taxi at first, which Nirmal's wife thought extravagant, and then as Mary grew alarmed at the mounting costs, by crowded bus and tram, which her companion, being small, found easier to manage than Mary. And always they were told that the key person had just left, or would be coming late, or that they should have gone somewhere else first, until Mary's relentless cheerfulness turned thin-lipped and suspicious. At one office where she waited for the third day running to speak with the person in charge, a junior officer observed her expression from behind his desk and commented with amusement, "The memsahib is cross with us today, I think!" Did they expect her to offer bribes? Should she comply? Reluctantly she enlisted the help of those who ran the guest house where they lodged. Eventually Mary was persuaded to pay a generous sum to an agent, who then produced all the necessary documentation within a day. Bribery at one step removed no doubt, but this was not the time to be scrupulous.

In the evenings they sat at a polished oval dining table, each place set with silver cutlery, and ate English food with the other guests. One middle aged couple, obviously newly married, the husband here on business, the wife surprisingly ugly when you looked closely, but you didn't look because she was so brilliantly witty and entertaining. An impatient young nurse on her way to East Pakistan, forced to delay her journey because relations between India and Pakistan were daily deteriorating. A most courteous elderly gentleman, gray faced and bald, always immaculate in suit and tie, who never revealed his occupation but talked with ardor of the village in Yorkshire from which he hailed. On the first day Mary explained to the assembled group that the Bengali housewife was not accustomed to the complicated etiquette of English mealtimes, hoping to put Nirmal's wife at ease by pointing out her inexperience. This proved unnecessary as she happily ate the food served to her, using knife and fork with confidence, and even practised a little English conversation with the nurse. She only excused herself from table if she heard her baby cry.

And when at last they loaded the single suitcase into a taxi and set off for Dum Dum airport, Mary was overcome with admiration for this woman, and wondered at her resilience as she sat watching the busy road ahead, clutching her baby to her side. This was the same boldness which had impressed Mary at Thanksgiving Wednesday all those years ago, when the shy young girl wrapped in pink and silver had assured Nirmal that she understood what marriage to him would involve, and that she still wanted to go ahead. Again and again during the last three weeks of broken appointments, endless form-filling and interviews, repeated disappointments, and the tedium of waiting rooms, Mary asked her whether she wouldn't rather return to her husband. And when they sat, idly waiting, and watched children playing round their bored mothers, Mary pointed out certain individuals, and deliberately drew comparisons in age or appearance to Sunil and Jayanti. Nirmal's wife was often upset, but her decision remained unchanged, she would not go back.

This consistency was what Mary needed. She didn't want Nirmal's wife to go abroad, no one would have been more pleased than Mary if she had asked to be returned to the school and her family. However, if there was no hope of reconciliation between husband and wife, then going to England was the best option for both of them and for everyone else (meaning for Mary herself).

But as they jolted and bumped towards the airport, Mary thought of how radiant Nirmal was the day he first met his bride, and then of Jayanti and Sunil's unsuspecting play the night their mother left them, and the conviction that had driven her through these three exhausting weeks began to unravel. Mary laid her hand with its spattering of brown blemishes and folds of loose skin circling each finger joint, over her companion's small firm hand with its blunt fingers ending in tiny half-moon nails.

"You alright?"

"I wouldn't say I'm alright exactly, Miss Featherstone, I was sick earlier and I still feel queasy because I'm terrified. But if this is my fate, if this is what God wants for me, then I accept it. I'll go to the place you've arranged for me and forget all about this country and what happened here. I must put all my energy into making a safe home for my baby, that's what I'll concentrate on." Now it was the younger woman's strength that kept Mary together, kept her from canceling the whole project, from ordering the taxi to turn round and drive back away from the airport.

CHAPTER TEN

1999

〜〜〜

Rupa is beginning to tire of the zoom lens thrust in her direction, the innocent inquisitions endlessly repeated and frank comments passed on every little thing she does. What at first struck her as honest intimacy conveying affection, has become unwelcome intrusion. They are sitting at table sharing a meal and thoughtfully turning over the events of the day, when an unknown voice calls from outside, crosses the veranda, and is sitting in the chair beside her before she realizes it. Or she comes out of the bathroom carrying a pile of dirty clothes, gamchha wound carelessly around her head, and finds Jayanti in her room waiting to introduce the visitor who's sitting on her, Rupa's, bed. Rupa knows they would judge it selfishness were she to express her discomfort at these invasions of her personal space. "Personal space" is an empty concept in the context of this household – even the cuddles and embraces of Priya and Bijoy are beginning to irritate her, not the physical contact in itself but its unrelenting nature. Her acquiescence is taken for granted, no one considers whether she might object. It would be okay if things were discussed, agreed to in advance; this preparation of banana flower, mocha as they call it, for the midday meal for example, realistically Rupa never had the option of declining to join in. It just wasn't possible to say, "Actually, I'd rather sit by myself and read."

Chhaya fetches a bottle of mustard oil from the kitchen and passes it around. Rupa, Priya, and Bijoy each pour a viscous yellow pool into the cupped palm of one hand and then bring the other palm down on top so that the oil is squeezed and spreads out. Then they massage the sticky liquid thoroughly into the fingers and backs of both hands.

"Rub it in well' Chhaya warns, "the juice looks clear but it can leave a black stain for days." The oil's pungent vapor stings Rupa's eyes. She recalls the way dandelion sap used to mark her hands after she set out a dolls' picnic, hollow stalks chopped up for food, yellow heads decoration for the tablecloth. Thinking of yellow flowers reminds her of Bijoy's marigold related exploits, and she watches him as he earnestly rubs oil into his hands before helping to cut up the banana flower. An unusual boy, quite content to be involved in women's work.

Rupa and the children are on the floor mat, Chhaya sits on a low stool bending forward so that her knees are level with her shoulders. She tears at the purplish leaves dulled by a powdery grayness, which clasp the banana flower, long and round and smooth, shaped like an air to ground missile. She rips back the tough rubbery outer leaves which overlap in a tight embrace, and places one of them, boat shaped, as a receptacle to receive the individual florets.

"Your brother loves eating mocha, I tell him it's a lot of trouble to prepare but still he brings one back from the bazaar whenever he can." Chhaya works as she talks. Under each leaf lie two tight rows of florets which she snaps off and piles onto a plate. The others take them one by one, stripping off the inedible transparent membrane beneath the head, and removing the wiry stamen. Priya shows Rupa how to do it, demonstrating the action while providing a lively commentary, and then gets Rupa to practice while she observes. When the upturned leaf is full of cleaned florets Chhaya takes a handful and slices them ready for cooking, using an upright blade fixed to a wooden base which she steadies with her foot.

"I can't remember what it tastes like. Does it have a distinctive flavor? It certainly looks different." Rupa's hands move slowly as she concentrates on the fiddly operation and Priya giggles at her clumsiness.

"Be quiet, you, I'm doing my best!" Rupa smiles back.

"Actually it doesn't have much taste at all, I have to use lots of cinnamon and cloves otherwise it's too bland. It loses its shape and color in the cooking process, and looks totally insignificant on the plate." Chhaya laughs. "It's the idea of it, as much as the real thing, that your brother enjoys."

The outer leaves have been removed now and the inner ones are glossy with a reddish magenta sheen, and more supple. They protect the flower so closely that each one has to be peeled back gently from the tip, and coaxed to give up its treasure. The florets toward the outside are fully formed, just beginning to turn brown, but those nearer the center are pale and soft like asparagus with golden faces. They cower at the base of the leaves, immature grubs hidden from the daylight, timid and yielding in Chhaya's hands. So soft that there's no need for any part to be removed. Bijoy has placed his own stock of florets on a separate dish and continues to work through them methodically, oblivious to the fact that the others have already finished.

Priya is bored. She goes into the room and sorts through her box of tapes until she finds the one she wants, a newly released collection of Nazrul Giti, songs by Kazi Nazrul Islam, the people's rebel poet. The cassette player is in Nirmal babu's room. He's sitting on his bed writing something on a sheet of paper which he hides under the pillow when Priya enters, then peers at his granddaughter, curious to know what music she's going to play.

"Did you know, Dadu, I've been asked to make up a dance for the children to perform in Church at Christmas?" Priya explains, her tone deliberately calm and patient as she anticipates his objections. "My mother bought me this tape so I'm going to play it through to see if any of the songs are suitable." Nirmal babu gets off his bed muttering anxiously and stretches clumsily round furniture to get at the window shutters which he closes, shutting out the light.

"Ooff! I'm only going to try out a few steps!" Priya is already annoyed. She plays the tape through, all the time guarding the cassette player from Nirmal babu who grows agitated and reaches for the on/off button whenever a deity's name, Ram or Krishna or Jagannath, is pronounced. The song she finally chooses hops and rebounds disjointedly in thin straight lines, no swoops no curves, light and brittle as a cricket, never settling, always just out of reach and escaping.

> *Where do you look to find Bhagavan?*
> *In the forests, on the mountains,*
> *In the temple, or the mosque.*

Priya experiments with a few jerky movements, all elbows and angles, toes and fingers crooked. Not like any dance Rupa has seen her dancing before.

> *Makka, Medina, Kasi, Brindaban*

At last Bijoy is distracted by the music. He stares in amazement at his sister's unfamiliar postures. "What are you doing, Priya didi? That's not the proper way!"

> *Examine yourself in the looking glass,*
> *Look carefully, for he dwells within!*

Priya collapses onto the floor exhausted by the effort of her originality. "Well you try then if you're so clever, but you've got to listen to the song and match the dance to it."

Chhaya has all but finished now. Right at the flower's center, leaves and florets merge into the same creamy color and share the same fragile texture so that they are indistinguishable, no longer separate entities. She tidies away the various utensils and passes round pieces of a lemon which she's picked from a tree in the garden. Rupa and Bijoy dutifully smear the juice over their hands. Mustard oil before and lemon juice afterwards, those are the rules. Bijoy accepts Priya's challenge and goes into Nirmal babu's room where he and his sister play the song over and over and argue about how best to dance the crazy mosquito tune.

Chhaya sits back on her stool and studies Rupa's face. "What did Mamima feed you when you went there?"

"Sweets and luchi when we arrived, then at midday so many different dishes, two dals, vegetables – I can't remember what exactly, at least three kinds of fish." Rupa smiles as she remembers the quantities of food offered to her. "But in their house it's not like it is here, with you having to do everything yourself, Mamima has such a lot of people to help. In fact I didn't see her do any of the actual cooking, only supervising the other women." Rupa can't believe Chhaya really wants to know this, it has to be a way into something else.

"Did you talk to her much?" Chhaya glances at the remains of the lemon wedge in Rupa's hand, and Rupa realizes she is absentmindedly shredding the peel with her thumb nails.

"I rested on her bed after eating and we chatted then." Is Chhaya ready to talk about her absent mother-in-law, or just curious to know how Rupa was treated at Poltu mama's house? "Mamima talked a bit about when Sunil dada and Jayanti didi were little." That should provide her with a cue.

"I thought there might be something on your mind. Since your visit there you seem preoccupied, a bit sad perhaps, as if something had happened there that disturbs you."

After all Chhaya is only concerned for her visitor's state of mind, not inquisitive about the family of the mother-in-law she's never met. It's unnatural, this detachment. Suddenly Rupa is overwhelmed by a fierce determination not to let this too cautious sister-in-law go on avoiding the family secret, the past which is her husband's and Nirmal babu's and Jayanti's past. Rupa can't see Ma but can feel a manic presence urging her to force this secret out into the open. Rupa hears her own rasping breath as she turns and ducks, her hands raised in an attempt to fend off the blows that attack her from behind. And it's all caught up with the insane tune coming from Nirmal babu's room where the children are rolling together on the bed, laughing hysterically. Chhaya stands up in alarm.

"Rupa, what's wrong? Are you feeling ill?"

"No no, I'm not ill. Sit down, Chhaya boudi, please sit down.

I really need to talk to you or Sunil dada, to someone anyway, about what I heard while I was at Poltu mama's. So yes, you're right, I have been worried, well troubled, by something that happened that day, something Poltu mama's grandson told me." Rupa feels weak and hollow with the effort but isn't going to back away from this now. Chhaya settles herself on the iron bed and pats the place beside her. "Tell me."

Rupa speaks quietly even though the music is playing too loudly for either Nirmal babu or the children to hear what she says. "Did you ever hear anyone say my mother left, or was sent away, because she was having a relationship with another man, an affair?" Saying this inside her own head was not so difficult. She's surprised to find it's actually painful to say the words aloud, their barbs scrape against her throat as she utters them and the wounds exude the foulness you taste when a tooth is rotten and needs filling. Calm as ever Chhaya responds immediately.

"I've heard that said, yes. I gather it's the explanation some people gave at the time, but I've no idea whether it's true or not. Your brother thinks it's true, Jayanti doesn't agree. I suppose only your mother herself knows the truth of it, and the other man if there was one." Chhaya's eyes, giving no hint of what her own opinion might be, gaze steadily, coolly, at Rupa, challenging her not to pursue the matter further. Her expression makes clear to Rupa that she won't allow anything to upset her family.

Rupa looks out into the yard, at the sturdy mango tree and at the greenly moldering bag of cement. So they all know of this rumor! Then why didn't Jayanti tell her on the day she arrived, when Rupa was asking her what she knew of their parents' marriage and Ma's exile? To protect Ma's reputation? Not if Jayanti doesn't think it's true. To protect Nirmal babu, because she thinks he made up the story to place the blame on his wife, while he retains the status of the injured party? But Jayanti told her Nirmal babu's story for these neighbors concerned a sick wife who was being treated abroad. Or to protect Rupa, because Jayanti does believe the rumor's true, and doesn't want Rupa to suspect that she's not Nirmal babu's daughter?

A woman's voice hails them from the gate to warn that she's

approaching. A sagging gray-brown sari comes round the corner, she stands casually on the lowest step and asks to borrow yesterday's newspaper. Chhaya calls a little sharply to Priya telling her to bring the paper from the pile under Nirmal babu's bed. Everyone is tense wondering whether there's something in it's pages that they've missed, more of the Pope's pronouncement or an editorial condemnation of his words, or further reports of attacks on Christians, anything to justify local hostility.

Priya switches off the cassette player and Nirmal babu comes out of his room to greet the woman, addressing her as "daughter," and asks about her family, her health, her husband's job. He sits down in his easy chair while she replies. She takes the paper that Priya holds out and perches on the veranda steps for a while looking through the pages, searching for something in particular. Chhaya crouches down and slowly tidies under the iron bed, in silence. No one looks at the woman but everyone's attention is wholly fixed on her bent head as she scans the thin typed sheets. She stands up suddenly and cheerfully hands the paper back to Priya, saying that she couldn't find the piece she wanted to read. Chhaya escorts her to the gate, leaving Priya and Nirmal babu to search through the outspread pages for themselves, relieved but still wondering what it was the woman had been looking for.

Chhaya restrains the children from following Rupa when she goes up to her room after eating, to lie on her bed and listen. Listen to the lazy breeze rustling palm and mango leaves, to the squeaking of a pump, the slap of wet clothes on stone, the rattle of an empty ricksha, the rise and fall of a hundred unself-conscious conversations and distant radio songs, the plaintive bleating of a goat, the explosion of an occasional fire-cracker. Rupa waits for sleep to come, like an orgasm, flowing quietly in from the horizon, not to be stared at or assisted because then it would slide shyly away, but to be recognized, breathing slowly, and invited to come nearer. Although warm drowsiness laps round the edges of the bed it doesn't flood over her because of the barrier put up by her agitated thoughts. Decide on an action and hang onto that, then sleep will come. As she drowns she is repeating over and over that she will talk to Sunil, talk to Sunil, talk to Sunil.

But it is Nirmal babu who wakens her. "Rupa, Rupa, can you hear me, are you awake?" He first calls and then enters the room, standing awkwardly for a minute or two before sitting stiffly on the edge of the bed, arms resting on his thighs, hands together, head slightly bowed. She sits up confused, her eyes not focusing, pulls her clothes straight and finger combs her tangled hair away from her face.

"I'd like to buy you a sari, a sari to wear while you're here and take back with you when you go. Any kind you like, but of good quality, probably a silk one. Jayanti will know what's best." He looks round and smiles widely at her, revealing long stretches of bare gum, and his eyes are sparkling in anticipation of her pleasure at his offer. To Rupa it doesn't feel like love, to be on the receiving end of his attentions.

"That would be nice, I'd like to have a new sari. We'll have to arrange with Jayanti when she's free to take me to the shops. Do you want to come too, to help me choose?" Don't tell him you never wear saris and don't want his gifts anyway, that this is all a sham because he isn't your father and he knows it.

Rupa is surprised by her reaction, after hearing Mamima's story her feelings should have changed. She thought she was beginning to understand him, even like him a little, but somehow she can't connect this man sitting on her bed with the sad figure searching for his wife, described by Mamima. She is ashamed. Face to face all her sympathies evaporate, leaving her standing in a murky puddle of guilt.

CHAPTER ELEVEN

Everything in the shop glitters and sparkles, from the gold designs painted on the walls above and beneath glass covered displays of hanging saris, to the silvered space-age egg boxes which spread out over the entire ceiling, each shining concave reflecting the row of tube lights a hundred times. Two of the walls are full from top to bottom with shelves, protected by sliding glass doors, on which are stored piles of folded saris, and in front of these spaced out at even intervals sit five salesmen, cross-legged behind a low counter. Rupa, Jayanti and Priya sit on chairs on the customers' side of the counter while Sunil sits near the entrance, chatting to the owner of the shop.

"What's your price limit, that's the first thing to decide, then we can see what materials and styles come within that range." Jayanti has responsibility for the conduct of this shopping expedition, and wants everyone to know she intends to carry out the operation with efficiency. From the doorway Sunil calls out that price isn't an issue, Baba will pay for whichever sari Rupa likes best. Jayanti is furious, of course price is an issue, if you let the salesmen know what Sunil has just revealed then there is no scope for bargaining. He's just ruined her whole strategy. Priya understands her father's mistake and glances at Rupa, trying to gauge whether she has realized what's happening. Rupa meets Priya's eye and winks. Frowning darkly, Jayanti begins again.

"Show us some of your best quality silk saris, not the old designs, something new and stylish. What color, Rupa, any preference?"

"Beige or brown, natural colors, nothing bright." Rupa wonders if she wants new and stylish or would rather have old and traditional, but isn't going to risk upsetting Jayanti again by saying so.

Jayanti looks puzzled and her frown deepens. Beige or brown? Her sister has no taste. One of the attendants reaches up with a long hooked pole to dislodge some bundles from the top shelves. A stretch of red velvet is spread out over the counter before the lengths of sari are unfolded onto it in order to do justice to their borders and decorative end pieces. Jayanti feels the different materials, testing them between thumb and fore finger, examines them for manufacturing defects, studies the patterns, holds the saris up against Rupa to see if they suit her complexion, discusses what colors could be picked out when it comes to choosing a sari blouse. Jayanti's not satisfied with the selection they've shown and asks to see something else, something unusual. Sunil is growing restless, chiding them good-naturedly to decide quickly or move on to another shop.

The owner gives an order and one of the attendants disappears and a moment later a hatch opens above their heads. A sari is lowered down into the hands of another attendant who stands on the counter to receive it. This time Jayanti is impressed and consults with Rupa who is tired and prepared to agree to anything, especially as she was never really interested in buying a sari in the first place. Everyone hopes the hunt is over, but just before paying the bill Jayanti asks for the parcel to be unwrapped and the whole length of sari to be opened out for her inspection. She finds a small dirty mark along one of the folds.

"You told me this sari was new, bought in for this Puja. It's an old sari. It must have been lying up there for a long time. Just look at this mark!" The owner promises he'll pay for the sari to be cleaned and have it ready for her to pick up the next day. Jayanti accepts the offer but wants the price reduced to compensate for the inconvenience caused to them. After a few words with Sunil the owner agrees. Then he insists they all drink tea before leaving his shop. While they wait for the tea to be brought from a nearby stall, he asks Rupa about clothes shops in England.

Rupa manages to arrange for Priya to travel back in Jayanti's ricksha while she climbs up beside Sunil. It's not the best place to confront him about his memories of Ma, but she rarely has a chance to be alone with him and isn't going to miss this opportunity. She's had some of her most productive interviews with clients while traveling in a car, sitting side by side you don't have to make eye contact, facial expressions can be hidden, your reactions concealed.

"Listen Sunil dada, I want to ask you something."

"And it's not about saris, is it," Sunil is teasing her but she won't be deflected.

"When I was at Poltu mama's house the other day I heard something about Ma which shook me, really surprised me because I'd never even thought of it before. I spoke to Chhaya boudi about it, I expect she told you what Poltu mama's grandson said?"

"No, Chhaya hasn't told me anything. You tell me, Rupa, what did he say?" Sunil's voice remains light-hearted, refusing to acknowledge Rupa's obvious emotion.

"He said he'd heard people suggest that Ma was involved with another man, who could have been a teacher, at least he thought so." It was easier this time, just a scratch in the throat and the bitterness of coffee grounds. "He didn't want to tell me but I persuaded him. You knew about that already didn't you?"

"I don't know anything but, yes, I have heard people say she was unfaithful. Not here, people here think she's seriously ill, but when we were still living at the school I was teased by children who said she had a lover." The ricksha bumps suddenly over a particularly uneven bit of road and Rupa grabs the rough metal handle to steady herself as the jolt throws her forward.

"And who did they say she was unfaithful with?" Carefully, no change in tone, continuing the conversation in the same tenor.

"I can remember at the time that Mr. Das seemed to be part of the problem. Come on Rupa, it all happened long ago, what does it matter now? Don't forget you'll have to go and pick up your sari tomorrow. Good choice, Jayanti's first-class at buying saris, don't you agree?" Sunil isn't going to make this easy, he will make her beg for every bit of information.

"Who was he then, this Mr. Das?" Not for nothing has she spent hours in police stations and juvenile courts.

"He was one of the teachers in Baba's school and used to come often to our house." Offhandedly, not really interested but needing to respond to Rupa's enquiry. "I don't really know why, but he and Ma used to get out lots of books and talk and write for hours while Baba was out doing tuition. Nice man, sometimes told us stories, Bible stories made enjoyable for children by adding fantastic and funny bits. I've told them, in the way he did it, to Priya and Bijoy."

And then looking at her in the dim streetlight Sunil laughs with just a touch of mockery, "What is all this, Rupa? You don't ask your mother about what happened years ago, why do you ask me? I was only ten remember, Baba didn't tell us why she left but she did leave and we've all managed well enough without her. Why all these questions? Are you an undercover reporter collecting material for an exclusive? No thanks, we don't want to be famous." He struggles to pull up the ricksha hood and huddles down as if hiding from Press photographers. The rickshavala looks round in surprise and stops pedalling. Sunil chuckles and waves him on.

"Developing the story line for a new television soap actually, with you as the villain." She is his youngest sister and can only make demands of him up to a certain point, Sunil's responses tell her that point has been reached. He's saying it won't help the family to delve into these past events and so her particular needs aren't up for consideration. It's always a question of balancing needs, child and parent, carer and cared for, employer and employed. Maybe he'd be more sympathetic if she explained her doubts over who her real father was. But not now, the moment has gone, and anyway even thinking of telling him sickens her and tingles all her joints. Mr. Das, a nice man who used to tell stories, funny fantastical stories, to children; she has gained this at least.

All along their homeward route pandals are being dismantled; skins of colored cloth are peeled away, planks which form steps and platforms are levered apart with jemmies then stacked on ricksha vans. Little boys circle the area like hawks, swooping every so often to pick up discarded nails which they hammer straight with blows from broken pieces of brick, before dropping them into plastic bags. Other children treat the bare bamboo structures as giant climbing frames, while men perch on horizontal poles patiently untying bulging knots, then sling the lengths of jute rope over their shoulders before descending to work on the next layer. Already the images have sunk to the bottom of local canals and rivers, in contrast to the figures in Christmas nativity scenes which are carefully wrapped and stored away to be reused the following year, a little shabbier.

A ricksha is parked in the lane ahead, and as they draw near they recognize it as Jayanti's. It has halted in front of Khuku's house, she's standing in her empty gateway, teeth protruding as ever in a broad smile. Rupa wonders what happens at night, whether she can draw her lips down to cover her teeth as she sleeps. Priya is recounting the tale of the sari hunt and has just got to the final purchase.

"It's an amazing design, you've never seen anything like it. Look, I'll show you." She bends forward to feel in Jayanti's bag and then she remembers. "Oh! I forgot, it's not here, it's in the shop waiting to be cleaned." The silliness of her mistake sends her off into peals of laughter accompanied by arm waving, head shaking, feet stomping, which delights Khuku who repeatedly asks Priya to show her the sari. "Where is it, where is it then Priya? You said you'd show me!" The merriment is infectious and the others make little amused noises in their throats and amused snorts down their noses.

"Come on, come on now, we'd better go home. Chhaya will wonder what's happened." Sunil's rickshavala stands on the pedals and maneuvers his vehicle out into the lane past the stationary one.

"Tomorrow the painters are coming to decorate the downstairs rooms," Jayanti explains to Khuku. "We'll have to take out all

135

the furniture and put it on the veranda so they can work inside. It's going to be chaotic." Rupa traces a note of pleasure behind Jayanti's announcement, she's relishing the challenge of this redecoration project.

The rickshas proceed in convoy along the lane, trying to keep their wheels out of the many grooves and holes, guided only by the window light from houses beside the way. Shadowy figures step back to the edge as the vehicles roll dimly past. When they get home Priya has to go through the sari story again for the benefit of Chhaya and Nirmal babu, this time adding, with revived hilarity, an account of their encounter with Khuku.

Next morning Rupa is woken by the loud declamations of a neighbor who complains to the world at large about the dirty water from next door's kitchen drain which is overflowing into her land. The woman makes this loud complaint every morning, accompanied by the regular swish swoosh as she stoops to sweep the flat area in front of her house. No one ever replies to her loud complaints, and presumably no action is ever taken to remedy the situation. Does she go through this daily ritual to ensure she starts the day in fighting mood, a kind of limbering up for the trials and tribulations which lie ahead? Rupa has heard the same words every morning since she arrived, and can chant them in unison with the neighbor, and with the same intonation.

Rupa emerges from her room to stand in the weak sunlight and look out through the trees into the garden and beyond, and then down onto the pump which Priya is working for Bijoy who fills his cupped hands with water to splash over his face, a comfortably familiar view. The morning birds are calling, a plumy alto wobbles on a single note, another rises thinly higher and higher working up to a climax but falling away as its courage fails, yet another produces the reverberating twang of a flexing saw blade, a metallic quiver. Rupa is startled to hear Sunil's voice call her name. The sound comes from the roof so she climbs the narrow stairs to see what it is he wants. He stands with toothbrush in hand, his back to the low wall, watching her as she crosses the roof to stand near him. He gestures towards the mango tree with his toothbrush.

"I planted that mango tree the year we laid the foundations for this house. At first it grew well, the soil hadn't supported any trees for years so it was full of goodness. The second year something checked the sapling's growth and it became spindly, only a few leaves, altogether a sickly specimen. I couldn't see any signs of disease, no one knew what was wrong with it although the neighbors all had their different theories, but we kept it watered and hoped it would recover. Now just look at it! Big enough for Bijoy to hide in, and it supplies us with a crop of fruit each year, so long as the storms don't destroy the blossoms before they set or knock the young mangoes to the ground before they ripen. Not an abundant crop but a reasonable one." He pauses to apply his brush vigorously to his teeth and then leans out over the side of the roof to check there is no one standing below, before forming his mouth into a circle and blowing out a frothy mixture of toothpaste and spittle, which dollops onto the ground below.

"Do you see what I mean? There's no point now in carrying out tests and investigations into why the tree didn't thrive for a while when it was young. If we did that we might actually damage its present health. It's doing well enough, so just leave it alone and enjoy its branches and shade and whatever fruit it produces." They are both silent for a while. The sounds of Chhaya preparing breakfast drift faintly up to the roof, the small sounds of kettle and stove and teaspoons and china. Rupa wonders whether Sunil lay awake last night composing this parable for her benefit. She is unsettled by this brother whom she doesn't recognize. Where is the humor that customarily circles his words, blunting the corners and edges of what he says?

"We missed her, of course we did, don't think because I told you to leave the past alone that we have forgotten, forgotten her, or how much we missed her. The smell of her beside us if we woke during the night, the sound of her calling us in the morning, her singing, her hands combing our hair, or pressing a little hollow in the rice on our plates ready for the dal to be ladled into. You've never known anything else but life in England with her, but we *lost* her." Another pause but this time no brushing of teeth, just a pause.

"If she hadn't gone Jayanti would certainly have married, Priya and Bijoy would have had a grandmother, two grandmothers in fact, and Baba a companion. Have you thought how lonely his life has been? You're alright, she's alright, living happily enough together." A change of tone. "Before long you'll find yourself a husband, and next time you visit us you'll bring a Michael or a John with you, won't you Rupa?" This is easier for her to handle.

"And the time after that Priya and Bijoy will play with the little Jacksons or Majors," Rupa responds smiling, playing his game, concealing any sign of the dreariness that settles across her scalp. Sunil nods and chortles, then resumes the assault on his teeth as he bustles over to descend the steps. His vest stretches tightly over his protruding stomach, and his toes point outwards as if to accommodate and balance its bulk.

Rupa stays on the roof her back against the wall, the sharp bricks on the top edge cut into her spine above the waist. It's her habit to take another's viewpoint seriously before rejecting it, so she considers whether Sunil might be right, what's happened can't be altered so accept it and appreciate what you do have. Of course the parable of the mango tree is fine from his perspective, but from Rupa's it has a serious flaw because her branch of the tree is not thriving. If she told Sunil this, he would laugh and say she was making a fuss about nothing, indulging in unhealthy introspection in the manner of pampered Americans endlessly visiting their shrinks. Maybe her search is a symptom of neurosis. She can recall a Pakistani tutor, during a session on Women's Issues (or was it Cultural Diversity?), saying that in her country no one mentioned the menopause as a medical problem, it was only privileged Western women who had the time and energy to be concerned with such things. Then Rupa remembers her tears the evening she returned from visiting Poltu mama's house, and knows with a crystal certainty that if she doesn't find out this time what she needs to know, then a few years down the line she'll be back again, asking the same questions.

Even supposing Sunil could be persuaded to accept that she's not flourishing, that her growth is stunted, it wouldn't alter much.

His advice would probably be akin to that offered by consultants to the parents of a disabled child. Never mind why it happened, defective genes or medical incompetence, look ahead and plan the future, prepare to help your offspring to overcome this handicap. But Rupa's intention isn't to apportion blame, to gather enough evidence to secure a conviction like the prosecution of Nazi war criminals and cold war spies, many of them old men (and women) like her father, forced to face up to actions they carried out too long ago. Nothing is achieved by condemning one of her parents as guilty, that would only make her relationships with both more complicated. Perhaps what she really wants is to effect a grand reconciliation, pretty unlikely in view of the lapse of time since it all happened.

So is Sunil right? What's happened can't be altered so accept it, and appreciate what you do have. Far too pious, much too wise. Rupa hears light footsteps, slow and careful, and then a small hoarse voice. Bijoy is coming to call her downstairs for breakfast.

CHAPTER TWELVE

While Rupa sits at the formica-topped table drinking tea and eating rooti and alu bhaja with the children, and Chhaya is busy cooking khichuri (rice, dal, vegetables all in together for speed), Jayanti is already preparing to clear the two downstairs rooms.

"Yes, Baba, everything will have to come out, it's no good doing the thing half-heartedly. They won't be able to work properly if stuff is left lying around, and anyway it would get splattered with paint. Apart from that, it's ages since anyone cleaned under your bed, no doubt we'll find a few mice and cockroach nests. This is the chance to have a thorough clear out. We might even throw some of the stuff away, what do you think?" Nirmal babu's low grumbles rise to more audible protests at this last suggestion.

Chhaya and Rupa exchange glances acknowledging that Jayanti is in charge of the day. She will organize and supervise and they will not challenge her, they will comply with her demands in order to keep the peace. Chhaya calls out to her father-in-law, telling him his water's ready. He emerges from his room with a muffler wrapped round his head against the light chill which feels to Rupa like the welcome freshness of a summer morning. Chhaya swivels round on her low stool to pass Nirmal babu the heated pot. He bends forward to take the vessel cautiously with both hands, holding it under the rim with a ragged piece of cloth. Nirmal babu knows Chhaya will protect him from this upheaval, rescue him from his bullying daughter if necessary. Rupa looks fondly at the children. At Priya, whose conspiratorial grin shows she has understood the way of things, the silent agreement between her mother and her pishima, and at Bijoy who is tearing the thin outer skin of his rooti into shreds, placing a fragment beside each oily yellow sliver of potato. She will occupy the children if they grow bored or get in the way.

"We can make a start with moving some of the stuff before the workmen arrive. Priya! Have you finished yet? Come on, I need your help."

"Wait one minute till I drink my tea. Just coming, Jayanti pishi, coming!" Priya stands up, pours a little water over her fingers, and hurries away, smugly satisfied to be the first one summoned to help. Bijoy scowls at his plate, despite the elaborate maneuvers with his food he has eaten nothing yet.

"Are you going to help too?" Rupa wonders if he's feeling left out.

"Maybe. I'm still eating."

"You're not eating," Chhaya laughs, "you're playing."

"I'm eating!"

Rupa goes through to stand on the veranda, reluctant to appear too eager, just watching and awaiting instructions. There are only a few days left before she must leave, why did they have to sabotage the last days of her visit by calling in the decorators? Couldn't it have waited?

Firstly the wall clock, its engraved brass plate announcing that it was presented to Nirmal babu on his retirement, is taken carefully down. Then the photos and framed biblical texts are removed from their nails on the walls, and handed to Rupa who wipes them clean of dirt and cobwebs and stacks them neatly with the clock on the iron bed. She notices that there are no photos of her mother, all the pictures date from after her departure, or from Nirmal babu's life before he married. Then everything else which hangs – curtains, calendars, empty cloth bags, oddly bulging nylon bags, water bottles, belts, mirrors, a discarded hurricane lamp, one of last year's Christmas decorations. Shirts and trousers thrown over the high wooden frame round Nirmal babu's bed, the frame from which at night his mosquito net is suspended. Various items stuffed into the rusty gaps in the window grills. Then everything found lying on a flat surface – bottles and tubes, tins and boxes, books and torches. Nirmal babu sitting in his easy chair, smokes and watches in agitation lest anything should fail to reach its allotted place amongst the growing pile of his possessions on the iron bed.

Jayanti's next category is everything on the floor under the furniture. Specifically under her father's bed of blackened teak, the beautifully turned legs of which stand high on bricks with the intention of providing more space for sweeping, but actually providing more space for hoarding. Rupa looks at the dark accumulation of broken shapes and thinks of it as one mass, the items no longer separate but stuck together layer upon layer by dirt, the whole woven together by cobwebs. If you pulled it by the corner the whole unpleasant mass would slide out as one, or at least trail out in a long line like the string of tin cans tied to the honeymoon car after a wedding. Nothing putrid, nothing festering, just the dry detritus of an old man's petty life. Not a matter for the masks and overalls of Environmental Health, rather a referral to the disposable gloves of Domiciliary Care. Jayanti, nothing daunted, is crouching down, disentangling one filthy object after another, passing them to Priya with instructions to pile them up in the garden, rubbish to be sold or burnt.

While Priya is busy in consultation with Jayanti, Nirmal babu quietly sorts through the debris and retrieves an old pair of shoes, a torn suitcase, a leaking bucket, things which could be mended. He conceals them behind the henhouse next to the beehives, to be rescued later and restored to their rightful position under his bed. Bijoy, peering round the kitchen doorway, sees what his grandfather is doing and runs to whisper loudly to his mother, who nods and smiles and lays her finger on her lips.

Sunil returns, followed by two workmen with their equipment which they unload from the ricksha van and store in the shade of the tree. Huge clay bowl, tall square tins, chunks of lime, rough jute brushes, and finer hemp ones for delicate work. Jayanti holds a conference on the veranda at which it is decided that Sunil and Chhaya will begin clearing their room while the workmen, under Jayanti's supervision, lift down the trunks from the concrete shelf just under the ceiling in Nirmal babu's room. The men fetch their black iron ladder and place it against the wall, a ladder with no hooks or angled feet or any safety features as far as Rupa can tell. She looks away as they struggle to shift the heavy trunks to the front of the shelf, tip them over the edge and lower them to the ground. She is convinced the ladder will slip and men and trunks will crash down to the crack and crunch of breaking bones, legs and backs. After the last trunk is safely brought out onto the veranda they pause, covered in sweat and dust, and bend to wipe their faces on their hitched up lungis. Half-jokingly they suggest refreshment, and Rupa willingly goes to make tea. Bijoy is dispatched to the Chhoto kaku's shop to buy (cheap) biscuits.

The workmen drink their tea and smoke their biris squatting down together in the dappled garden out of sight. Rupa, sitting on the veranda steps, listens to their crude, uninhibited banter and wishes she could join in. She tries to imagine their expressions if she strolled along to join them, lit up a cigarette and settled down to contribute some crudeness of her own. In the house she is suffocated by the grubby intimacy of so many personal effects, smudged finger marks round handles, dribble stains on pillows, hollows worn in mattresses. Witness to the endlessly repeated movements of someone else's daily life.

The veranda is crowded with furniture now, and Nirmal babu sits miserably surrounded by jostling cabinets, tables, chairs, clothes stands and a steel almirah.

"Are you there Baba? Have you had your cup of tea?" Sunil pretends he can't find his father so that Bijoy can clamber over slopes and ridges and finally proclaim, "Here he is! Here's Dadu! I've found him!"

Chhaya makes her way towards them, brushing cobwebs and dust from her neck and shoulders as she weaves her slim figure through the clutter. With one foot she indicates the row of trunks lined up below the window grills. Casually she asks, "What about opening those before they go back on the shelf again? I can't remember what's in them, can you Baba?"

Rupa turns her head idly, curious to see what the trunks look like in full daylight. She gasps, and shivers, as she watches frenzied hands scrabble to draw back the bolts, stubby fingers with boat-shaped nails trimmed painfully short. The others continue to debate whether or not the trunks should be opened, Chhaya is gently persuading Nirmal babu that it would be a sensible thing to do. Rupa is convinced there is something inside one of them Ma desperately wants her to see, so she adds her support to Chhaya's efforts.

"Come on, let's open them! I want to see what Baba's stored away in there." Spoken with enthusiasm and feigned jollity. Nirmal babu leans forward, rigid, staring at the bolts. Then he raises his eyes to meet Rupa's and she knows he too has seen the fingers, has recognized his wife's hands. He sighs and his body relaxes, as if in resignation. He gazes steadily at his youngest daughter, a naked gaze which says, "I surrender, you've done it, the two of you. She's led you at last to the truth."

"Alright, why not? Let's open them and see what's there." As he speaks Nirmal babu keeps his eyes on Rupa's face. There's no meanness in his look, he's just waiting to fulfil his obligation. It's his duty to explain, he wants to explain. In some ways it will be a relief. His eyes reassure Rupa – *it's not so terrible, you don't need to be afraid.*

Sunil fetches a piece of brick and knocks the first bolt from its rusted bed, then he works it back and forth to loosen it, and repeats the process for the second. At last the lid is forced open and propped against the rough wall behind. Chhaya presses a handful of sari to her nose to block out the smells of sour metal and naphthalene balls as she stretches out her other hand to disturb the trunk's contents. Dull brass plates, bowls and glasses lie in sullen rows across the surface. These must be Nirmal's marriage set, long ago replaced by stainless steel, so light and shiny in comparison.

"No wonder it's so heavy!" Chhaya wriggles her hand in deeper between the hard planes and curves, and draws out a pinch of cloth between two fingers. The color's faded, though a tinge of pink still lingers in the folds.

"Move the plates to one side and then you can get at it properly.

144

There's a notebook wrapped in that cloth, I'd like to see it. Pass it to me would you?" Rupa is puzzled that Nirmal babu's voice is thoughtful, calm, whereas her own heart is pounding. If this really is the crucial revelation, then where's the drama, grief or anger or whatever?

Chhaya eases the bundle from its nest and holds it out for Nirmal babu to take with grateful hands. Tarnished silver strands untangle as he removes the wrapping.

CHAPTER THIRTEEN

Jayanti is invited to come too but, annoyed that they're abandoning their work, she will not leave her post, so only Rupa and Sunil go with Nirmal babu to hear his explanation. (Perhaps it's not her style in any case, to sit humbly at her father's feet and listen.) Carrying the notebook and assuming the same dignity he displayed during the incident of Haldar babu and the missing marigolds, Nirmal babu leads them slowly up the stairs to where they can talk uninterrupted. Giggles bubble up in Rupa when, to relieve the tension of their somber progress, Sunil winks at her. He unrolls a thick mat on the floor in front of Jayanti's room, and steadies his father by the arm as the three of them take up their positions. Nirmal babu is in command of the moment as if pausing for prayer before embarking on a public address. He lovingly turns the pages of the notebook which is loosely covered in brown paper, tattered and torn along the edges.

"It all began with this notebook, if I hadn't seen it that evening I might never have known." Quiet for a moment while he briefly considers this possibility, before dismissing it with a shrug. "It was your mother's notebook, I'm sure you've both guessed that. Her handwriting, neat and undeveloped like a child's. Would you have recognized it?" He smiles while he speaks. His fingers continue to caress the pages as he holds out the notebook for them to see. Rupa leans forward to check, frowns and shakes her head.

She only knows how Ma writes when she's writing English. Sunil nods but doesn't move.

"I found this notebook on the bed one evening when I came back from tuition. We were living in family quarters at the Mission School, you know, and I gave tuition most nights. My salary wasn't enough to provide for the needs of a family, now that we had three children I'd taken on more evening work. It meant I wasn't in the house enough, I couldn't keep an eye on everything." Rupa wonders what he means by that, what did he need to keep an eye on?

"Anyway, she wasn't in the room when I came in, she'd taken the baby, I mean you Rupa ..." he narrows his eyes to contemplate her for a while, as if trying to connect that baby with this young woman, "... taken you into the other room for some reason, to clean you up or change your clothes." Rupa is jerked away from her musings, transfixed by his words, suddenly finding herself in the center of the drama.

"She left the notebook lying on the bed, I suppose she didn't think I'd be home so soon, otherwise she'd have put it away somewhere secret. A thick notebook full of her handwriting, so I knew she'd been working on it for quite a while." This is surreal, thinks Rupa, he's talking about his wife's handwriting, and what we want to know is why our mother is in exile thousands of miles away. Wait a minute, could this be the diary in which Ma recorded the details of her infidelity? Will he let them read the evidence for themselves first hand? Could they bear to?

"She must have kept it hidden deliberately, because this was the first time I ever saw it. She never showed it to me or told me what she was writing, although she was busy with it for months. She didn't do things without telling me first, without asking my advice, of course I was angry, resentful that she'd left me out!" Now he's almost shouting, Rupa knew his composure couldn't last, the emotions will erupt as he relives them. He shakes the notebook roughly and drops it onto the mat in disgust, as if it's unclean. Sunil leans forward on the point of saying something but changes his mind and lets his father continue.

"And then I looked at the pages properly," having regained control, Nirmal babu resumes his narrative. "At first I didn't understand; what she'd written sounded familiar but I couldn't quite recognize it. The words were different. I soon realized that they were Bible stories, but dressed in the wrong clothes. Not in children's language like we used to do for school, but in common Hindu words – words which have no place in our Bible." He spits this out like a snake ejecting poison, and slams his fist into the notebook to emphasize his words. Rupa is alarmed, the violence of his anger frightens her. Sunil puts out a hand to pacify, but recoils as if his father's body is electric.

"I don't suppose I read it very carefully then, but I did notice some pages were written in an unfamiliar hand, weak backward sloping letters." His lips curl into a snarl. "I shouted to your mother to come and explain. I was furious." Nirmal babu picks up the notebook and hurls it against the low wall which it hits and then slithers to the floor, its spine broken, pages splayed out crookedly like an injured bird. Rupa wants to pick it up and cradle it in her arms, a glance at Sunil tells her not to move. She knows he's thinking, but won't say, "I told you so."

Nirmal babu breathes heavily for a while then looks up at Rupa apologetically. "You've seen me irritable, complaining and bad-tempered, but never furious. I used to have a terrible temper though. Sunil knows." Sunil smiles dutifully at his father, raises his eyebrows and nods in agreement but says nothing. Like Rupa, he's trying to guess where all this is leading.

"Anyway, she came when I called. She was embarrassed and didn't want me to see what she'd written. She tried to take the notebook from me and I pushed her away, I didn't strike her, just pushed her away." The words come slow and deliberate, matter of fact and dispassionate, recalling the actions in precise detail. "I put my hand on her shoulder, under my palm I could feel the double thickness of her blouse neckline, and I shoved her backwards I remember it exactly because I'd never done that before."

"It's alright, Baba, it's alright. You've told us enough, you've said all you need to say. You don't have to go on." Sunil is uncomfortable with this confession, he doesn't want to hear any more. Why drag all this up again? But Nirmal babu doesn't want to stop.

"She said the writing was something she and Mr. Das were working on, and that they planned to show me later when it was finished. That really maddened me, Mr. Das knew and I didn't!" The words come rapidly, projected by his rekindled anger. "Why did she share her ideas with him and not with me? Who was he for goodness sake? Someone who happened to have taught her for a while before her confirmation. I knew she liked his lessons, I knew they got on well. He was often in our kitchen talking, eating, laughing with her. But this, to work together for so long and not share it with me...." Nirmal babu bows his head, hiding his face behind trembling hands. Great shuddering breaths are followed by groans drawn up from some dark place deep inside.

Although she is moved by the sight of her father weeping, has indeed to swallow her own tears, at the same time Rupa doubts his sincerity, despises him for losing control. Sunil, glad to be doing something, goes down to fetch his father's cigarettes. Rupa expects to see him return with Chhaya in her role of comforter, but is mistaken. Sunil returns alone. Hearing footsteps below, Rupa looks into the yard and sees Chhaya with the children hurrying away in the direction of the bazaar.

"She tried to explain but I didn't let her," Nirmal babu is determined to continue. "I wouldn't listen. I was yelling, screaming at her to get out, to go to Mr. Das if he was more important to her than I was. She tried to tell me she was doing it for her family ... which meant her parents and brothers, they weren't her family any more, I kept telling her. She said she was doing it so they, 'her family,' could understand the stories, she said they couldn't read our Bible, it wasn't good enough for them." He sneers in mocking imitation of her excuses.

"Why couldn't she just love us, me and our children, wasn't that enough? Why did she have to pull to one side all the time? She could have taken my hand and followed where I led, I wasn't going to harm her, she was my life. The more I tried to show my love, the more she pulled away. It tired me out steering a straight path while she fought to deflect me." He turns abruptly to glare at his son. "I warn you Sunil, Priya will do that to her husband if you don't manage her better. Letting her do whatever she likes, such wicked ideas!" Sunil smiles sheepishly and shakes his head but offers no reply.

"I still think your mother was wrong, completely wrong. It was through her marriage to me she gained salvation, couldn't she see that? No! She had to go back to her former ways. What I saw was Hindu words polluting our Bible stories, I saw my religion insulted by her family, I saw my wife corrupted by Mr. Das, and I hated what she'd written and I hated her," Nirmal babu's voice is saturated with untreated venom.

Rupa finds this both painful and bizarre, how can he mix discussion of religion with an account of the breakup of his marriage, speak of Bible stories in the same breath as the reasons for Ma abandoning her young children? Is it his way of camouflaging the truth, or is he attempting to rationalize what happened? Can he not see that families, personal relationships, are governed by their own logic and necessity, that religion only distorts these emotions. If things had been different she would have challenged him, as it is she can only listen.

"She didn't actually go till the next evening. I think she was hoping I'd have calmed down over night, but I hadn't, I was still angry, still shouting. When I came back from school I still wouldn't speak to her, except to tell her to get out. She waited to see if I would change my mind. Why should I change my mind? She hadn't changed hers. When finally I came home, later in the evening after doing my tuitions, she had gone, and I didn't care. I guessed Miss Featherstone knew where she was but I didn't want to know." Pronounced with defiance.

"And later, when I did try to find her, when my stubbornness had crumbled and turned to grief, and I realized I might never know my youngest daughter, by then Miss Featherstone had disappeared. She took extended leave, I heard much later she was working in a school in the South." Now his voice is weaker, and he rests his weary head in wrinkled hands. Rupa struggles to restrain herself from reaching out to him. *Not yet, my love is not so easily bestowed.*

"I went to my father-in-law's house, but they wouldn't help. Poltu dada told me they'd heard about the trouble between us, but he said they hadn't seen your mother and didn't know where she was. Who knows if he was telling me the truth? I thought, if she wanted to come back she would get in touch somehow, but she hasn't, so that means she's really gone. I knew she could be as stubborn as I was, and much tougher. Tough enough to walk out on her children if she thought that was the only way. And I decided it was finished, and I wouldn't think of her or talk of her again."

All three study the pattern of the mat on which they sit, triangles and diamonds, no soft edges, each tracing his or her own thoughts along the lines of color, deep red and dark green. Thoughts submerged for far too many years.

Rupa's back aches and her left foot is numb. She straightens her legs out in front and lifts her hand to examine the soft flesh at the base of her thumb where the woven strands of matting have left their mark. Nirmal babu continued to talk for some time before Sunil took him downstairs, exhausted and clutching pathetically at his son's arm. Rupa's thoughts have absorbed all her energy so that she has not been able, until now, to move her body. She draws up her legs and wraps her arms around them, fitting each elbow into a hollowed palm. Resting her chin on her knees, she rocks slightly from side to side while she continues to think. As she considers Nirmal babu's account, for the first time she sees herself distinct from Ma, like a double exposure emerging where before there was a single image clearly focused.

So it was all down to a sordid little quarrel which could have been sorted out in no time, she would have referred them to a marriage guidance counselor. Sordid because it involved her father's weakness, his jealousy, his physical rage. Not that Ma was innocent, she had kept her idea a secret, knowing very well he would be hurt by that secrecy. It's obvious from the way Baba narrated the story, and from what Rupa heard at Poltu mama's house, that he was still in love with his wife. How fully that love was reciprocated is less clear.

It was so trivial, so stupid, and then later so stubborn. And what was it actually all about? A translation scribbled in a notebook! Okay so Rupa realizes that language and culture and identity are closely bound up, but for goodness sake, we are talking here about a married couple both Bengali, both Christian, who have three young children. How could they let this incident send half the family into exile, leaving a son and a daughter to grow up motherless? But isn't that often the way, a combination of minor tensions and unresolved complaints, ignited by a single event into an explosion with disproportionate consequences. She'd hoped for something more definite, easier to grasp, a cause significant enough to justify the ensuing pain.

Mixed in with her frustration and disbelief Rupa recognizes something else, a vague disappointment at having lost the shadowy romantic figure who might have been her real father. A form emerging in the sky which, when you looked again, has dissolved as clouds drift in the wind. Perhaps it was never more than that, a white smudge in a gray sky. In contrast Nirmal babu had grown, filled out, solidified as he told his story, a process which began when Mamima described his tearful search.

While her father spoke Rupa had seen him walk into his family quarters sweating, thirsty, hours of teaching echoing through his head. He reaches out to pull his lungi off the clothes stand when suddenly his eyes are trapped by an unfamiliar notebook tossed casually onto the bed. He's puzzled, then suspicious, and when he turns the pages, angry. He flings the lungi back onto the stand. Gripping the thick notebook he shouts to his wife, his shouts come from the same throat that has patiently instructed and explained all day in school. Rupa warms to this man, shares his anger at his wife's dishonesty, can almost forgive his pride.

When Ma hears him call she knows at once what he's found and frantically seeks for a way to explain, to make him understand how excited she is about her writing, what pleasure she gains from it. Does she take the baby with her as she hurries back into the room? No, most probably it's left alone well away from the battleground. What follows isn't very edifying, her parents' maneuvering, accusation and defence, attempts to wound and to placate. Their refusal to back down, their extreme obstinacy.

Abruptly the rocking stops. The thought kicks her in the stomach even before her brain has had time to process it. Who says the shadowy figure has gone away, Nirmal babu's version of events doesn't have to be true. Maybe the quarrel wasn't just about some scribbling in a notebook, and that's why the story was too smoothly told, wasn't quite convincing. Maybe Nirmal already had cause to suspect his wife and Mr. Das shared more than friendship. That would account for the violence of his fury.

Rupa pictures it again. This time the notebook is tucked between the pillows, still warm from the hands of someone stretched out and at ease, someone who has been reading with deep pleasure. When he examines it more closely Nirmal recognizes Mr. Das' handwriting alongside his wife's, confirming his already strong suspicions. Rage at this humiliation blazes out of control. When she hears him call, Ma panics and searches desperately for an excuse, anything to steer him away from questions about her relationship with Mr. Das. That's why she over-emphasizes her passion for the translation. That's why her husband screams at her, and orders her to leave. This version is more credible, but is it true?

Rupa's muscles relax, hands slip to the ground, knees move apart and her head falls backwards so that she can see only evening sky, gray cloud streaked with pink discreetly pulled forward to cover Earth's face. She abandons the effort of ordering her thoughts and allows them to leak into one another, losing their separate shapes and levels, like deliberately letting your eyes lose their focus on a printed page until the lines run together and slide diagonally into crisscrossing chaos.

Jayanti has woken up late, and is still recovering from the stress of organizing yesterday's redecoration. She went to bed exhausted but satisfied at having seen the work successfully completed. Being preoccupied with more important matters at the time, she ignored the discovery of the notebook and her father's subsequent confession, but now she's hungry to hear everything, every word that was said. So Rupa has relayed a full account, some of it quoted almost verbatim (she has a flair for accurate recall), some of it glossed with her own interpretations.

Jayanti emerges from the bathroom wearing a loose housecoat which hides her shape, until she bends or turns and the cloth tightens over bulky hips and stomach. Even then no intimacies are revealed, only a rough outline, for she wears both petticoat and blouse beneath the garment. Rupa sits on a bamboo stool enjoying early sunlight on her closed eyelids. She's carried up two cups of tea, carefully positioning her feet on the steps, toes turned a little inward to avoid tripping on the hem of her long skirt, and placed both cups on the table in her sister's room.

"Did Baba explain why he'd kept the notebook? If it was me, if I was that angry, I'd have burnt it." Jayanti fetches another stool and Rupa hands her one of the teacups.

"He said he kept the notebook as evidence of her treachery, and something with which to confront Mr. Das, although he said he never actually got round to confrontation. He would take out the notebook and look at it to fuel his anger and remind him why he sent her away. That was at first. Later when he realized what a terrible waste it was and wanted her back but couldn't find her, then he looked at the handwriting with longing because it was her writing, after all. He tore out the pages on which Mr. Das had written, wrapped the notebook in one of her old saris and kept it as a memory. You should have heard him, Jayanti didi, he spoke movingly, full of sorrow, like a poet."

"Sentimental rubbish," Jayanti grunts. "So he's absurdly jealous and accuses his wife of being disloyal, just because she asked another man to help her work on an idea. Hits her ... alright, pushes her roughly ... and tells her to get out. And when she finally goes, well then he's sorry and wants her back. And because he can't find her he gets all soppy over the things that remind him of her. Nothing poetic in that!" For a moment Rupa is stunned and then she bursts out laughing. Soon Jayanti's expression of disgust melts into a grin and she laughs too.

"Tell me though, what's all this about polluting the Bible by translating it in a way her family would understand? Would that be enough to make him so mad?" Rupa is serious again. She wants to test the plausibility of Nirmal babu's version, judge whether the explanation he offers is consistent with his actions.

"Ridiculous. Paranoid. Why shouldn't she do that? It's just more of his obsession with separating everything into Hindu or Christian, instead of seeing some things as just Bengali. To answer your question, yes, it would seem to him like deliberate provocation, crossing the boundaries he had set. That's what this is all about, he wanted to control her, even her ideas."

Raising a hand to shade her eyes Rupa watches her sister's face, and sees no signs of the distress which was evident on the day of her arrival. That first conversation when Jayanti demanded, no begged for, personal messages from Ma. Now Jayanti is comfortable with her mother's part in the story, confirmed in her opinion that her father was at fault, reassured that her mother was not guilty of leaving her son and daughter willingly. It's not how Rupa sees it, not so clear-cut, so black and white at any rate. Once again she is aware of a gap opening up between herself and Ma, the doubly exposed image is fast becoming two distinct pictures.

They hear the sound of Sunil's cycle bell grow louder as he comes down the lane at the side of the house and into the yard, to be met by Bijoy jumping down the veranda steps and shouting excitedly, "He's here! Baba's back from market!" Sunil dismounts and holds his cycle upright, calling to Priya to come and help unload the bazaar bags which hang off both sides of the frame behind the seat and from the handle bars, the weight evenly distributed. Sounds of the children's footsteps accompanied by Sunil's gentle admonitions to take care, convey the progress of unloading to the two sisters sitting quietly upstairs drinking tea. Suddenly Chhaya's voice explodes.

"What, you've bought lata fish? How am I supposed to clean it, tell me, tell me! Look Priya what a brainless fool your father is, he's brought lata fish for me to cook. He thinks only of himself. Because he loves eating lata fish he goes ahead and buys it, not sparing a thought for the person who has to clean it. Hey you, come here and look! See, it slips out of my hand! I can't hold it still to get the scales off. See, see, it's slippery just like soap. You can't grip it without using ash, and I don't have any ash. We use gas to cook, or haven't you noticed? Where am I going to get ash? Tell me, tell me then, how am I going to manage? Yes, very nice, he wants to eat lata fish. What bad luck I have, to marry such an idiot."

For an instant the house stops breathing, everyone stops. Then Jayanti and Rupa rush to look over the wall down onto the yard where Sunil stands transfixed, his position indicating that he was just about to wheel his cycle round the back. Priya comes running up the stairs, her eyes wide with surprise, her cheeks flushed, and looks from Jayanti to Rupa and back again as if seeking an explanation. Chhaya, kind diplomatic Chhaya, has never had an outburst like this before. Rupa notices Bijoy creep towards the mango tree and stealthily pull himself up till he's shielded by leaves and branches. Sunil leans the cycle against the side of the house and goes towards the kitchen. They can hear his voice, cajoling, teasing, chiding, employing every tactic to restore calm. He calls Priya downstairs, and sends her round to the neighbor's to say her mother needs some ash so she can clean the fish her father's brought from market. Nirmal babu shuffles through to see what's going on.

"Strange! In fourteen years I've never heard Chhaya boudi do that." Jayanti looks puzzled, lifts both hands and twists her wrists in a gesture of non-comprehension. "Obviously it doesn't suit her to think that her father-in-law is guilty. She's been very loyal to him, always maintained it must have been Ma's fault."

Jayanti goes into her room to take down the mosquito net. Colored strips torn from the border of someone's worn out sari stretch from loops at each corner of the net to hooks in the wall. She unties the strings, neatly folds the net (not an easy task because of its three dimensional shape) and pushes it underneath the pillows. Then she covers the lot with a brightly patterned bedspread, and smoothes out any wrinkles using the short sharp strokes of a small stiff brush kept under the edge of the mattress. Rupa thinks, no I can't leave it at that.

"Sunil dada thinks Ma was having an affair, doesn't he, and

that was why she had to go away. Why didn't you tell me about that rumor, Jayanti didi?" Rupa's voice is flat and gray.

"Because I didn't believe it, nasty spiteful gossip." Jayanti's is highly colored.

"It would explain why she left though. I'm not quite convinced by Baba's story, there must have been more to it. It doesn't seem possible, just because of something she wrote." A persistent almost peevish whine.

"It wasn't what she wrote, it was his jealousy, narrow-mindedness and wicked temper." Jayanti wearily, patiently, as if explaining to a child.

"But to go away for ever, to leave two children and her parents ...." Rupa stands in the doorway and whispers the words, trying to recapture the enormity of what had happened.

"He told her to go, remember," said Jayanti defiantly.

"Come on, I'm sure she didn't do everything he told her to," Rupa protests.

"Perhaps in the end she knew that if he didn't want her as she really was, then she didn't want him."

Very profound, thinks Rupa. Yes she can imagine that. Ma has fended off insulting comments about her family, negotiated all sorts of restrictions on what she does, but this is different. The translation is her creation, it seems to express an essential part of her, and now he's spoilt that too. Up till now she's been supple and resilient, like a branch that springs back each time when the weight which burdens it is removed. This time the weight is too great and the fibers of wood are tearing. If she doesn't escape, the branch will split and never heal. There's no choice, she simply cannot stay. As Rupa said before, a combination of minor tensions, unresolved complaints, growing resentment, because of some catalyst, in this case the finding of the notebook, spirals out of control.

Rupa drags herself back to sit behind the judge's bench. On the other hand, pursuing the alternative theory ... Ma knows that she and Mr. Das have been found out and she is ashamed. She wants to spare her son and her daughter that shame, let them say she is ill, better a mad absent mother than a present bad one. Perhaps she's thinking of her husband's reputation. It's the same thing, in this country scandal and shame belong to families not individuals.

"The crucial question is this, why did Baba go in search of Ma? When I was at Poltu mama's house, Mamima told me he went there, quite distraught, to look for her. Did he realize he'd been fiercely possessive and come to beg forgiveness? Or to beg her to come back in spite of her adultery, because he loved her so much?"

Jayanti's back is to the door, and she doesn't reply. Instead she takes a broom of shredded date-palm leaves and begins to clean the floor with long smooth sweeps, panting from the effort, her loose housecoat billowing out in a huge bubble below her arching body. Let Rupa pursue her investigation, Jayanti wants no more to do with it, for her the matter's settled. What agonies Ma must have suffered, forced to leave without her son and daughter.

Rupa collects the cups and carries them downstairs, past the empty brooding bowl, to the kitchen where Priya sits hunched up on a low wooden stool listening to her mother's scolding. Priya rubs the tip of her nose on the palm of her hand and sobs noisily. On the floor in front of her is the offending item, an enamel dish piled with small potato chunks which should have been long wedges.

"I told you what to do, I even cut one to show you how to do it, and still you get it wrong! Will you never grow up?" Chhaya has her back to Rupa. Water from the bucket sloshes onto the floor as she fills the cooking pan, and as she empties rice impatiently from the bazaar bag into the storage tin, precious grains scatter like confetti.

Going to the door to chuck a handful of peelings out into the yard for the hens, Chhaya catches sight of her son who has climbed down from the mango tree and is anxiously watching his mother and sister while he pees on the solidified sack of cement.

CHAPTER FOURTEEN
1999

Mary Featherstone is wakened at five by honeyed trills and cadences, a sweet blessing indeed. Dear Lord, may her hearing never deteriorate to such an extent that she can't rejoice in a spring dawn chorus. Such a colorful time in the garden, without opening her eyes she conjures up each hue. In the long grass groups of daffodils in every shade from light cream to deep gold, in the borders grape hyacinths like bobbley blue ices on green sticks, along the front wall blossom covered branches pointing straight to heaven as if gigantic skewers have been first dipped in glue then rolled in heaps of white petals. Beside the path ivory magnolia flowers tinged with crimson, rude and arrogant on bare branches, nor has the forsythia any green leaves amongst its yellow stars. The neighbor's copper sycamore (is it a maple?) is dotted with leaf buds which, from a distance, look like sticky toffee apples, the tops nibbled away to reveal the fruit's pale flesh. And yesterday the sounds and smells of lawns being freshly cut. While sitting in the gentle sunlight she'd noticed the rhubarb in her vegetable plot, and must remember to pick the first pink stalks (thereby stimulating the plant to put forth stronger thicker redder stalks), and make a pudding with brown bread crumbs, grated orange rind and cream.

Usually she dozed off again but this morning Mary remains firmly awake because her mind is full of train times, lifts and trolleys. The taxi's ordered, that part of the journey's been taken care of, but managing her bags (up escalators, over bridges, onto luggage racks), the stiffness and swelling in her joints makes that difficult. However there's no other way now she's been forced to give up the car. Last time she went to a college reunion (how many years ago was that?) she drove there and back for the weekend, no problem. Now she's in her eightieth year and it has to be the train, so she'll make the best of it. Swapping tales with other passengers, listening in to mobile conversations, looking through smutty panes of glass at business men, couples, families waiting on platforms. It was all so interesting, a way for someone of her age to keep up with ... with the modern world.

Mary raises herself on her elbows and slides her legs until they hang over the side of the bed. She sits for a while on the edge to allow her blood to circulate, and looks with disgust at her feet, the big toes grow diagonally, passing over their smaller neighbors in a grotesque manner. She tells herself it doesn't really matter, she's the only one (apart from her chiropodist) who ever sees this old age deformity. On the positive side, the publicly visible portions of her legs are still shapely, with not a hint of varicose veins. She stands up, hides the offending feet in slippers, and crosses the landing to the bathroom where she turns on hot and cold taps simultaneously. Each bath has its own particular quality, the serious "after gardening" scrub, hasty "before Church" dip, relaxing "on return from holiday" soak, and her favorite the "after guests leave" reflective ablutions. This morning it'll be a "last before I go away" bath.

Having successfully deciphered the "Departures" board and negotiated the step up into the correct coach, Mary finds her seat without any bother. What makes other people so pathetic? Hesitating for ages beside a seat, repeatedly checking their ticket against the reservation tag, unable to decide whether or not the two correspond. She intervenes to assure one such fainthearted traveler that this is his seat, but he's still not convinced and persists in hovering uncertainly in the aisle to the inconvenience of other passengers. Let him hover, she doesn't have the energy to try again.

Doors slam, a whistle shrills and they begin to move, casting loose from platform and station. Ridge tiles on the roofs of houses sag in the middle, like the backbone of a cow sags under the weight of its swollen stomach, while the cottage gable ends, like bony hips and shoulders, strain to keep the ends apart. A row of squat industrial chimneys stark against the skyline, their thick smoke rising in parallel lines as if choreographed. The train picks up speed, bushes close to the track flash past without ever looking her in the eye whereas trees in the distance grow a little familiar before they take their leave.

But mostly Mary watches the sky. Difficult to describe. White sand sprinkled onto a blue surface and feather brushed. White iron filings scattered aimlessly across the heavens and drawn into swirls with a magnet from the other side. Foam dances on advancing crests and thins out on the blue shore as the waves recede. Later the clouds become heavier and more varied in texture. Wedges of solid glacier behind frothy ice creams, and here and there a dirty gray smudge, a trick her mother had taught her when she first learnt to paint with watercolors. Use your thumb to smudge a cloud in the still wet sky.

Things had changed at the college of course. There had always been people from overseas living there while they studied for degrees, but now these seriously academic "study partners" formed the majority of residents. There were far fewer missionaries (sorry "mission partners") going out from this country, and those who went only did so for short stretches. No lifetime service as in her day. In Mary's time only women were admitted, ordained ministers were considered automatically qualified for mission work by virtue of the time they'd spent in seminaries. The training given to these women was designed "to equip them for the front line of the Christian army in its warfare with the forces of darkness!" That's how their Lady Principal had explained it, though it wouldn't do to talk like that today and Mary wouldn't want to. In the modern world the forces of darkness are not only to be found in far-off countries, a fair number can be seen lurking at home, even behind church doors.

There's time to doze, the journey's long enough, but please

don't let her dribble or snore, or sleep through the guard's inspection of tickets.

Mary's "station stop," as the train manager insists on calling it in his broadcast announcements, is the train's final destination. She waits until most passengers have disembarked, then smiles brightly at the boy wearing a black T-shirt (why do they all wear black, it's so unflattering and dull) sitting opposite, who seems not to have realized the train has come to a halt. Having caught his attention, Mary asks him to extract her suitcase from the gap between two rows of seats where it is wedged. He removes his earphones and asks her to repeat herself. Mary laughs aloud and her pale blue eyes water with amusement.

"Silly me, silly me! I didn't notice you were wired up. Now can you hear me? I can't imagine what damage it's doing to your ears but never mind, you're young and won't pay attention to anything I say. You look like a strong young man, would you please be so kind as to lift my case down onto the platform for me?" The boy hesitates and glances at his own bags piled on the seat beside him.

"What's the matter? You think I might run off with your luggage while your back is turned?" Her eyes twinkle and the boy flushes pink, not sure whether to swear at the old lady or apologize.

"I was only thinking I couldn't manage your stuff as well as mine. I'll put yours outside first and then come back." Gripping her suitcase with both hands he waggles it from side to side to loosen it, then struggles with it to the doorway and down onto the platform, trying desperately not to let Mary see it's too heavy for him. She follows him closely as he staggers along the aisle, so he has to wait until she's painfully lowered herself onto the platform before he can get back into the carriage to retrieve his things.

"Thank you, thank you very much. When you've fetched your bags you can take me to the taxi stand." They move along the platform. "Look mine's got two little wheels, very clever, I can manage it myself on the level." Slowed down by frequent collisions, they pass through the huddle of passengers standing, necks craned, in front of the "Departures" board. At last, to the boy's relief, they come out into the gray daylight beside a row of waiting taxis.

162

"Weird," he mutters, and raises a puzzled eyebrow at Mary who is waving energetically to him through the window of her vehicle as it pulls away.

Her bedroom is right at the end of the corridor on the top floor under the eaves, complete with slanting ceiling. Fortunately the lift, which has recently been installed thanks to the generosity of the Friends of the College, is only a few doors away. Mary remembers this room as the Sick Bay, it was the only room in the building with an attached bathroom and toilet, so could be used for patients who required isolation. More recently it has been used as a Poustinia, a desert cell for those making their Retreat. Today it's just another guest bedroom, though probably the grandest in the College, allocated to Mary in recognition of her seniority.

At supper Mary shares a table with a couple from Sri Lanka. She's finishing off an M.A. in Pastoral Studies and he's come to spend a term in College with his wife. Their youngest child, who is accompanying his father, sits in a highchair placed between them. One by one, with dexterity and great concentration, the infant picks up bright green peas from his dish and throws them gleefully into the air. Most land on the floor, some reach the dining table, one rolls onto Mary's plate. The child's mother is engrossed in discussion with a fellow student, his father stares blankly at nothing in particular as he chews each mouthful. It's no good, she can't just sit by and do nothing.

"That's no way to treat your food! Food's not something to be played with, people are starving out there you know. Let's see if I can feed you with this spoon." As Mary gets up and goes round to the high chair, the mother's eyes follow her and her mouth assumes a polite smile.

"Don't worry about him, he has little appetite but eats enough to sustain him. Please sit down and get on with your own meal." She speaks slowly and evenly, a woman accustomed to exercising authority.

"But I do so *hate* to see food wasted. I thought he might do better if he was given a bit of attention. You're a lovely little boy aren't you. Hasn't Mummy shown you how to use a spoon?"

163

Perhaps she shouldn't have interfered, but what kind of a mother ignores her child at mealtimes? A working mother, that's the problem. A mother who leaves her baby and travels halfway round the world to further her own career; a mother who is neither bothered about how much her son eats, nor about teaching him good table-manners.

People are looking in their direction, the general murmur of conversation has subsided. The child's mother lifts him out of the highchair onto her knee and resumes her conversation while he finger feeds himself from her plate. Mary cheerfully resumes her seat. During the rest of the meal she pulls comic faces to amuse the child when he's eating, and frowns and shakes her head at him when he messes.

After supper she goes into the Common Room to pour herself a cup of tea but doesn't stay because the television's turned up too loud. Instead she wanders down the corridor and finds a comfortable chair in the main entrance hall. From the chapel comes the rhythmic strumming of a guitar. It's tricky lowering herself into the chair while holding a full cup, they should have provided a coffee table. Nearby is a stand containing leaflets and brochures describing courses offered at the College, the usual thing, a colorful mixture of text and illustrations. Mysterious symbols and catchy descriptions designed to entice you. Mary finds her reading glasses and browses through the College Prospectus.

Liberation Theology (she's heard of that, it comes from South America and has a Marxist bias), but these others ... Black Theology, Dalit Theology, Minjung Theology, Feminist/Womanist Theology, Third World Theologies, Third World Feminist Theology. What's the point, why create all these divisions? Aren't we supposed to be "one body?" How can there be more than one theology? In his Epistle to the Galatians, St. Paul writes of breaking down barriers between Jew and Greek, male and female, slave and master. Why build new ones? As Mary impatiently returns the booklet to its place on the stand, someone, presumably the guitarist, comes down the chapel steps humming as he walks.

"Hello there! I'm Mary, I don't think we've met. Tell me, which courses are you studying?" The question is a challenge, an accusation, as if he's already confessed to taking one of the newfangled subjects mentioned in the Prospectus.

"Hello, Mary. No, I don't think I've seen you before. Are you here for the reunion?" He stoops to shake her hand, pressing it affectionately between his palms for longer than is necessary. "I come from Ghana and my name is Charles. I'm registered with the Center for Inter-Faith Studies, busy writing up my dissertation."

Next morning former missionaries are invited to attend a workshop, which is being run for anyone in the local area who's interested. A public relations exercise. Mary goes along but doesn't care for the style of leadership, college staff adopt an understanding and patient mien. If controversy develops keep your eyes cast down to avoid confrontation. Don't get heated or involved. Tolerate all viewpoints and remain calm. After coffee, participants are instructed to split into pairs to explore the topic in more depth. Mary has trouble focusing, while she listens to her partner speak, her thoughts race ahead. To avoid interrupting, she has to find a quiet cove in which to tread water until the speaker catches up. Not too quiet a backwater though, otherwise she starts pursuing her own new ideas and fails to notice the other person swim by on the way to the next phase of the discussion. When it's Mary's turn to feed back to the group embarrassed shuffles greet her outspoken remarks, and staff exchange cautious glances.

Nothing has been organized between lunch and tea, Free Time according to the program, which some spend dozing in their rooms. Free Time indeed, at Mary's age the urgent need is for time to be occupied, having not enough to do is so tiring, as exhausting as walking at a toddler's pace. She goes into the garden to watch and listen to the trees. There used to be an orchard in which she, as a student, spent hours picking fruit for Cook to stew and bottle. Little sign of it now, almost hidden under tall nettles and vicious brambles. These days more bricks than trees, a block of flats for student families, a whole new wing made up of conference rooms and offices, and on the far side a cosy bunch of staff houses. Material developments which increase college efficiency and income no doubt, but where is the passion, the sacrifice and dedication of her day? The God whom Mary married is her strength and joy. He gives her a life of hardship and adventure, picks her up by the scruff of her neck when she stumbles and showers her with blessings when she continues on the way. Yes she makes mistakes, fails at times to discern His will, and He forgives her with such generosity.

For some reason, this weekend Mary finds herself thinking repeatedly of Nirmal and his family. Like the fungus which causes athlete's foot, memories of the Nirmal saga have lain dormant beneath her skin, to break out again many years later. Perhaps the Sri Lankan woman who left her children with their father while she came to England, has aggravated the condition. Or the mission partner with whom she talked at breakfast, he described a recent meeting with Mr. Koshy, now a wealthy man returning to South India after an exemplary career in the Middle East.

Mary had kept in touch by visiting whenever she came home on furlough. Rupa's mother seemed to have established herself admirably well, with a permanent job and the tenancy of a terraced house situated in a pleasant area. Sadly the daughter was a disappointment, a clinging, whiney child. Intelligent maybe, but sickly and extremely timid. This disturbed Mary who cherished a desire to do something to help. She planned, when she retired, to take Rupa to concerts, historical sites, museums and art galleries, even perhaps an educational trip to Europe. So when she finally resigned and went to live in her parents' cottage (which was desperately in need of renovation and repair), Mary contacted Rupa's mother and invited the child to spend the summer holiday with her. The answer was "No, thank you." No valid reason offered, just that it was inconvenient, they were both too busy. By then Rupa must have been eleven, starting secondary school, conscious of her unusual family situation and beginning to speculate on the reasons for it. No doubt Rupa's mother wanted to protect her daughter from the stories Miss Featherstone could tell. At any rate they'd never met again, although Mary continued for a while to send a card at Christmas.

Does she feel guilty about what happened, does she regret arranging the marriage in the first place? No, she doesn't blame herself, she couldn't possibly have known they would give up so easily, would fail to make the necessary sacrifices and adjustments. The idea itself was good. But yes, she had felt responsible for mother and daughter when it all went wrong.

It's growing chilly and her joints ache from sitting too long in the same position. Mary pulls the folded program from her handbag but can't read it without her spectacles, puts the paper down beside her on the garden bench and delves into the bag for her glasses case, then has to grab the paper again quickly as it flaps in the breeze. Never mind. Tea and cakes at four, she's sure about that. Whatever follows, she'll willingly take part.

CHAPTER FIFTEEN

Mary would have preferred to come before autumn set in, but Rupa's mother postpones their meeting so often, that summer turns into piles of sodden leaves and invitations to community bonfires and firework displays before the two women finally settle on a date. The driver gets out to hold open the passenger door against gusts of rain-soaked wind, while Mary eases herself down from the taxi onto the pavement, shuffling to the very edge of the seat and stretching her legs to avoid placing her feet awkwardly in the streaming gutter. He offers to guide her through the gate and up the path in case she slips on the wet flag stones, but she declines. A woman is standing in the doorway, fumbling with an umbrella.

"Don't worry, it's far too windy! I'll be inside in a jiffy." Mary raises a hand in greeting and sets off up the path. The woman comes out a little way to meet her.

The parquet flooring in the hall glows under its new layer of polish, but the wallpaper bears the marks of fingerprints where someone steadies themselves to remove their shoes, pauses for a moment before entering the front room or turns to ascend the stairs. The paper has begun to peel off in little curls above the skirting board, and separate along the seams where the cut lengths join. Horrid wallpaper, bright orange embossed with furry thistles. What awful taste! Rupa's mother shows Mary to a chair in the front room and takes her damp raincoat to spread over the radiator.

"Terrible weather. I hope you haven't caught cold, Miss Featherstone. Sit here by the fire. I'll make us a hot drink." That's a relief, her English is fluent. Mary had not relished the prospect of dredging up her long buried Bengali.

The perfumed smell of polish from the hall fills this room too. The furniture is out of date and flimsy, nothing of any value. Lacquered and adorned with fancy scrolls and piping, stuck on afterwards not carved. The sort of stuff you'd find in second hand shops used by those on low incomes, not in the antique shops patronised by young couples with two jobs who are looking for a bargain. Mary knows all this because she's preparing to move out of her parents' cottage and has received offers for their furniture, most of which is solid oak and genuinely old. She's been round junk shops and auction rooms researching the market price for dining chairs and tables, sideboards and wardrobes.

She notices a framed photograph jostling with a heavy glass vase of plastic flowers, a china cherub painted pink and yellow and a cheap metal ash tray, for space on the mantelpiece above the gas fire. A young woman dressed in sparkling evening wear smiles into the camera.

"Surely that's not Rupa, this photo on the fireplace?" Mary calls through to the kitchen.

"Yes, that's her. I took her to the studio for a present on her twenty-fifth birthday. I was very pleased with the picture. It's a lovely photo isn't it?" Rupa's mother brings in two cups (not mugs, Mary appreciates that) of tea, and a pretty little plate of assorted biscuits. She puts down the tray and hands Mary the picture to examine more closely. Artificially posed of course, nevertheless the woman is most attractive, elegant and self-contained, a hint of humor in her eyes.

"I can't believe it! As a child … how she's changed. Will I see her later, when does she get home from work?" Mary passes the picture back, chooses a chocolate biscuit and raises her cup to her lips.

"She's away on holiday, won't be back for another fortnight."

Rupa's mother replaces the photograph decisively, as if dismissing the topic, precluding further discussion of her daughter. She lifts a stack of newspapers and magazines from the other chair, drops them carelessly onto the carpet, and sits down, leaning forward attentively as she waits for Mary to speak.

The whine of machinery from the factories in the back lane seeps via the kitchen into the room where they sit, interrupted at intervals by a metallic clatter. Cars pass by the front window, the sound of their engines altering at intervals as they slow down to negotiate speed ramps in the road. The clip clop of high heeled shoes draws nearer, then retreats, as a young woman teeters past on the other side. Two elderly Sikh gentlemen, colorfully turbaned, argue in loud Punjabi as they take the opportunity now the rain has stopped, to saunter towards the shops around the corner. Mary is unexpectedly silent, she who chats easily with anyone, produces effortless small talk.

"Please have another biscuit, Miss Featherstone. Let me top up your drink. The tea must be cold by now."

Why had she been so determined to visit? Mary tries to recapture the urgency she felt when she first suggested meeting, back in the Spring after the College reunion weekend. She had expected to fall at once into a series of "Do you remember when ..." and "Did you hear what happened to ...?" To assuage her need to share the past with someone who knew it first hand, once more before it was too late. A sense of unease, a fear of things she didn't understand, needed to know before she died. Yet she felt unaccountably shy. There was no weak spot, no way out of this cluttered little room with its satisfaction and completeness. Rupa's mother reappears with a teapot and pours hot liquid into both cups.

"You're working with old people still, aren't you, but not for the Council. No more cheerful armies of Home Helps. I think you told me you're employed by a private agency? She'll start with the known and work sideways to where she wants to be.

"Not just elderly, disabled too. More personal care, less housework, supposed to be a different service for each person. I enjoy it, it's my life, that and the things I do for Church. I could

170

retire next year but what would I do all day? The same kind of work I expect, perhaps as a volunteer in some Day Center. May as well continue getting paid!" Rupa's mother laughs and with one hand pushes back the twist of gray hair which hangs over her forehead, with the other hand she pulls out a hairclip, then replaces it, trapping the stray strands.

"We run a Day Center in our Church Hall. Very friendly setup, though I never could see the point of Bingo. We've recently introduced 'Reminiscence Therapy,' a fancy way of saying we encourage everyone to relive the past." Who could have guessed it would be so easy? "Someone brings in suitable materials, ration books, clothes, household bits and bobs, old photographs, anything that'll bring back memories. And we play records, music touches even the most resistant souls. It's specially good for those on the borders of dementia, apparently."

"I've heard of groups who run sessions like that," Rupa's mother nods and looks curiously, suspiciously, at Mary.

"Of course success depends on people sharing the same experiences, they stimulate each other. For someone like me who's lived so many years outside Britain, or someone like you who came here as an adult, it wouldn't work so well, would it?" Mary's head slumps forward and she stares into the heat of the gas fire. Rupa's mother reaches out to lay her compact hand on the larger wrinkled one with its shiny inflamed joints, and squeeze it gently.

By the time they've eaten the fish and chips (saturated with oil, don't think about it) and consumed three quarters of the apple pie (readymade and tasteless), they've worked through most of the staff at the Mission School, the servants and the pupils. Described the time when the local police, wielding lathis, were called in to control enthusiastic parents at Prize Giving; laughed at the student from Cambridge whose stubborn rash was a mystery until Mary discovered he'd never thought of rinsing the soap out of his clothes after washing them; shivered at the thought of the caretaker who loved to demonstrate how he caught mice by stamping on them with bare feet; marveled at the memory of monsoon storms which, in the space of a few minutes, turned the central school courtyard into a swimming pool three feet deep. Mary proceeds with caution, checking the reaction whenever a new name comes up. Avoids any reference to Nirmal, Sunil or Jayanti of course, but why on earth does mention of Mr. Das provoke such a dramatic response?

"I was talking to someone recently who met Mr. Koshy last year. He did well for himself I gather, came home wealthy and respected, having gained a reputation for honesty and leadership. I confess I often found him unapproachable, no sense of humor." Mary carefully eases her wobbly chair back from the tiny kitchen table. "Is it alright if I sit in the front room for a while, digest that lot before I phone for a taxi?"

"You don't have to go just yet. We'll have coffee, there's a box of chocolates under the television." Rupa's mother follows her into the other room and stoops to turn up the gas fire. "I approved of Mr. Koshy ... a clear thinking man, more interested in doing the job properly than whether people liked him or not, I appreciated that. I'm pleased to hear he's led a successful life." A simple remark thoughtfully delivered, or was a deeper meaning intended? She can't possibly know Mr. Koshy's true opinion of Mary's part in her marriage to Nirmal.

It has been fun, this conjuring up of incidents from their shared past, redrawing the details of characters partially forgotten. They've both enjoyed it. Yet the omissions, the people and events they've skirted round, now demand attention with an even greater urgency. Mary as she used to be would have posed the questions, would have accused Rupa's mother of pride or maybe cowardice, would have insisted on a full confession as a necessary precedent to healing. Today's Mary is learning to compromise, to accept that in this world nothing is complete. Or perhaps she's just grown lazy, drowsy from the artificial warmth and a full stomach.

When Rupa's mother carries in two coffees, she sees Miss Featherstone's head hanging to one side crookedly. She puts the cups down on the glass-topped table and arranges a cushion over the back of the chair so that it supports the old lady's twisted neck, then reaches for the chocolates before seating herself comfortably in the other chair. How strange to watch

Miss Featherstone at rest. When she's awake her face is animated, laughing, exhorting, scolding, never still, never expressionless even in prayer. During the fortnight they spent together in Calcutta so many years ago, not once had Miss Featherstone withdrawn into herself, excluding her companion, in spite of the obvious strain. Now her mouth hangs slightly open, corners drooping, and her eyes have disappeared amidst the sagging folds of skin.

During those two weeks Rupa's mother too had remained firm, refused to explain the cause of her husband's anger or discuss her reasons for leaving. Nor has she spoken of them since, ruthlessly assigning those memories to a separate category, a closed compartment. She refused to contemplate the images which rose repeatedly before her eyes, she deliberately turned her head away, concentrating instead on the welfare of her one remaining daughter. She told herself Sunil and Jayanti would soon learn to blame and so to reject their mother, this would quickly close up any gap resulting from her absence. She heard a Chinese proverb once, defining a wise man as one who controls his thoughts as precisely as an archer controls the flight of his arrows, and that's what she had done. Systematically removed all trace of her past from her daily thoughts, rather as an addict attempts to cure herself of her addiction. Starved of attention, the memories have shrivelled up and lost their potency.

Today over lunch she decided to take a risk, for Miss Featherstone's sake, to indulge the old lady's desire to wallow in the past. Their shared reminiscences have dissolved the dividing walls between this life and that, and here in her front room memories multiply. She calls to mind scenes not mentioned over lunch. Miss Featherstone's driver, acting as messenger between the female teachers' rooms and the bachelors who live in the engineers' quarters opposite, his uniform pockets stuffed with cigarettes given in payment. Engineers who hang out of their balconies late at night and gawp at their correspondents as they undress for sleep, standing too close to windows whose curtains are not fully drawn.

Mr. Das visiting the married quarters to work on the notebook, choosing his time with care, waiting until Nirmal has gone to the bazaar or is busy with tuitions. She flushes at the thought and lays a hand against her neck to cool it. Mr. Das had been a friend throughout her married life, naturally they grew fond of one another. She liked him straightaway, right from the time Nirmal first introduced her, a new bride anxious to fit in. Mr. Das (she always called him "Mr. Das" in mock formality, to preserve his status as a teacher) sat near her when she attended Church, guiding her through the service while Nirmal was intent on his own devotions. When he instructed her in catechism and commandments she was cheered by his enthusiasm, his sense of humor, even when taking classes he never grew too serious. Like a brother she treated him, offering affection and sisterly advice.

He continued to come frequently to their quarters over the years, to discuss school business with Nirmal, and on occasion to help with household errands if Nirmal was especially busy. He loved playing with Sunil, later Jayanti too, and she liked the way he behaved with children, not teasing and dismissive like most grown-ups. Both of her children enjoyed Mr. Das's stories, Sunil would block the doorway refusing to let him leave until he told at least one tale.

Each time he visited he came in search of her, watching while she made tea and sharing with her whatever currently occupied his mind. Uninhibited, spontaneous. She felt sorry for him eating in the Mess, so would fry a quick paratha and serve it with spoonfuls of evening dal and bhaja, followed by a little homemade chutni to sweeten his tongue. They were roughly the same age, whereas her husband was much older both in years and outlook, and seemed at times more like a guardian or an uncle. When he surprised them in the kitchen they were like two naughty pupils, he the schoolmaster. She can see the three of them so clearly, can see now what she didn't notice at the time, the pain Nirmal suffers on being excluded from their intimacy.

He had no grounds for jealousy, not then, it was only after they began writing in the notebook that her relationship with Mr. Das had changed. Mr. Das understood instinctively what she wanted to achieve and why it mattered to her so much. When they worked together on a passage it was as if he saw the final painting before she finished the rough sketches, and gradually she realized her excitement was more than pleasure in the beauty of what they wrote. Whenever a visit was due she would linger for a moment as she passed the mirror, run a hand over the hair smoothed back from her face and release a few curls to nestle round her ears, pull her sari tight across her chest to accentuate the mature curve of her breasts.

As she recalls these feelings, so precious and yet sinful, Rupa's mother presses the backs of her hands against her flaming cheeks to cool them. She'd been married for more than ten years by then, but never experienced this exhilaration, this powerful interplay of ideas and senses. Their ideas soared and swooped together through the hot air like colored paper-kites, and his fingertips on the page were to her as if he touched her skin. The project began soon after her third baby was conceived, and in her imagination a bond developed between the baby's slow growth in her womb and the progress of their literary creation. It sounds crazy now, well who knows perhaps she was a little insane. At the mercy of her raging hormones.

She notices the tremor in her hand as she reaches for another chocolate. The figure oblivious in the chair, is snoring softly.

Her intentions were honest. She passionately desired to share her new religion with her family, introduce her parents and brothers to the stories and wise sayings. Simply reading the Bible wasn't enough, for the book appeared to them like a stranger of obscure speech and customs. How she longed to breathe into it new life. When she tried to explain her idea to Nirmal he admonished her, she remembers the conversation well. Nirmal patting the place beside him on the iron bed, insisting she sit and listen while he explains carefully and at length. He tells her Scripture is meant to be difficult, to be pondered on and wrestled with. Think of Muslims reciting the sweet Arabic of the Koran yet understanding little, he says, or of Brahmin pujaris chanting mantras for worshippers to whom the Sanskrit makes no sense. How much more homely is the Christian Book! Yes, she replies, but she wants Moses and Jesus to speak as her father and brothers speak, and she wants Rebeka and the Samaritan woman to draw water from Bengali village wells. She is amazed as she recalls the passion she invested in her ideas.

So she said nothing more to Nirmal, but was delighted to find in Mr. Das someone who shared her impatience with the stiff and weary language of the Bible, who was inspired by the same desire to create something different, more vivid and immediate. And all along she knew that what they did was dangerous, so when Nirmal found their notebook she was overwhelmed with guilt, and judged her feelings for Mr. Das to be as wicked as the imagined deed. Didn't it say in the Gospels, she reasoned, that even to look at another person with lust was to commit adultery? How quaint that morality sounds to her now!

Thus far Rupa's mother has covered familiar territory, but if new questions arise she won't flinch from examining them. For instance, she hasn't previously considered whether Mr. Das was also culpable, she was too pre-occupied at the time with her own guilt. Surveying it now from a distance she's convinced he must have guessed how she felt, and is humiliated, realizing he understood what was happening and yet didn't stop. No, that isn't fair. She was a responsible wife and mother, not an innocent young girl. His actions were no worse than hers, he dealt dishonestly with a respected friend and colleague, she deceived a devoted husband.

Her breathing is constricted, this part doesn't flow so easily. She has to struggle not to turn away, but having started she must pursue the thought. Yes, Nirmal had adored her, taken care of her, and at first she was warmed by that protection, but as time went by and she grew more confident and could have fashioned her own life, his concern for her became an invisible cage. Everything outside School and Church was forbidden. No, that's a bit strong, rather the world beyond was painted dark and scary, to be feared and if possible avoided. At home she used to go where she liked, talk with anyone willing to listen, say whatever came to mind, surrounded by sunlight. After her marriage she was allowed out of course, but Nirmal chose where she went, he imposed restrictions. At first she was patient, hoping he would gradually loosen the invisible chains. Instead he seemed to find new ways of choking her. She was discouraged from visiting non-Christian families in the township, he stopped Sunil joining in the fun at Holi and prevented Jayanti attending dancing classes. Slowly, and this she found most difficult to bear, he cut her off from her father's household, daytime visits only, no overnight stays, and later she had to go alone, leaving the children behind.

Why couldn't he have bent a little, been less rigid? She pointed out to him that Jesus ate with sinners and tax gatherers, sometimes she felt she understood his religion better than he did himself. Nirmal could have indulged her spirit of adventure, her need to discover and try out things new and unfamiliar. After all it was this spirit that enabled her to contemplate marriage to him in the first place. She regarded it as a precious part of her character and could not have survived in England without it. She has to admit though, she now sees the value of Nirmal's firm adherence to what he'd been taught, his quiet consistency. What seemed dull and predictable, she would now call safe and reassuring. Ironically, now that she's free to, she doesn't stray much into the wider world, in practice her life is confined to her job, her Church, her daughter.

Her eyes are drawn to the framed photograph admired earlier by Miss Featherstone. When her daughter was eighteen Rupa's mother contacted the Missionary Society who used their ecclesiastical connections to track down the family in India. A visit was proposed, and having secured the family's agreement, a Society official kindly organized the journey. This was the best Rupa's mother could do to compensate for the years of silence, and she vainly hoped it might be the end of the matter. On her return Rupa was given no opportunity to talk, to tell her mother what she'd done, who she'd met or how she felt. The rules were not relaxed. How could she have been so cruel, so cowardly. Airmail letters began arriving, not many, two or three a year, but she never commented, never touched them. The fragile blue rectangles lay where they fell on the polished floor until Rupa picked them up. And when Rupa comes back this time ... how much longer can it go on? She gazes sadly at the photograph until the image blurs and she has to draw the folded hanky from her pocket to soak up the tears.

Forgive me, my wonderful daughter, flesh of my flesh. Forgive me.

Through the patio doors the wind tugs at the tall pampas grass standing moth-eaten and forlorn in the center of the garden, relic of a more ostentatious horticultural age. Rupa's mother wonders, as she wonders every year, why the plant leaves it so late before revealing its glory. The creamy feathered plumes unfurl just when the autumn storms gather in their fury, already most of the stems have snapped in two so that the plumes lie gray and sodden on the lawn. Like the pampas grass, she has waited too long.

The figure in the chair stirs, one foot twitches, eyelids flicker. Rupa's mother frowns suspiciously. Why did Miss Featherstone come here today, to mull over the past, or, being near the end of her own life, to urge her to act before it is too late?

"Now where are those chocolates you were talking about? I think I'm ready for one, soft center please." Mary is awake. She lifts her head and holds out a hand, smiling in anticipation as she removes the fragile silver paper from the strawberry cream which is obligingly placed on her palm. "That's something I really missed in India, chocolates after Sunday lunch."

Rupa's mother goes to make fresh coffee and book a taxi to take Mary to the station.

CHAPTER SIXTEEN

The only time Rupa hears a phone ring is during one of the television soaps. At midday the larger than life characters invade the neighborhood, watched by everyone who owns a television set or can catch sight of one through an open door or uncurtained window. Dramatic quarrels, passionate weeping, slushy violins and other sound effects echo through the hot sleepy air, amplified from all directions in volume and intensity. Rupa, feeling heavy and slightly intoxicated after eating rice, lies on her bed and drifts in and out of the illicit love affairs, malicious scheming, and fatal heart attacks.

Now Rupa needs to find a real telephone. Sunil has been to Calcutta to check the details of her return flight and there are some changes which she should let her mother know about. The best way is to make a phone call, telegrams are only for emergencies. None of the nearby houses has its own phone, though you can make local calls from the sweetshop by the ricksha stand. Nearer the center of town some of the wealthier households have private lines but they can't get an international connection. According to Sunil there is a booth beside the main market, beyond the point where their lane crosses the National Highway. Rupa should be able to phone England from there. He's never used it himself but knows of someone who has, to contact a brother in America, but won't do so again – you won't believe how much it costs for just three minutes conversation! Priya knows the place because she passes it on her way to dancing class, and offers to take Rupa there. Bijoy pleads with his mother to let him go too.

They set off together, both children self-conscious but proud to be seen with the pishima who lives in England. When Priya's friends call out to her she giggles and shouts back, catches hold of Rupa's hand and keeps on walking at an even pace.

"Hey Priya! Where're you going?"

"Oh just down the road."

"Have you heard, there's no school tomorrow. Ganguly madam's retiring so she's given us a holiday."

"I know. Mita told me."

Priya is happy to show off her visitor, but isn't going to share her. Bijoy marches forward looking straight ahead, ignoring the children who stop their games to stare and nudge each other and call out to him. A group of young men on cycles emerges from the gloom. They ring their bells and snigger as one calls out rudely, "Hello Madam!" Rupa isn't quick enough with a suitable response. Bijoy glares at the path in front.

She suggests a game; she'll begin a story and they must add to it, turn by turn. The tale of travel and exploration (Rupa), ghost and rakkhosh (Bijoy), hidden treasure and stolen babies (Priya), totally absorbs them, so that only Rupa notices the curious attention they attract from others on the lane. Priya scares herself and clings to Rupa in mock terror, Bijoy almost stumbles into the ditch as he demonstrates how he fights off the devilish fiend. Then they reach the National Highway and hold hands as they wait for a gap between the lorries that hurtle over the pitted surface, horns blaring, engines roaring, chasing the pale beams cast by their headlights until they disappear into the dusk.

Someone has painted "BJP the enemy of civilization" on a low wall beside the road. High up on the side of a building a poster declares that Bartaman, a daily newspaper, "Fears no one but God." Priya points out a small ISD signboard above a doorway and they climb the steps and enter. A skinny lady wearing glasses, and a thin shawl over her printed cotton sari, sits sternly in one corner of the room which has been given up for use as an office, though there is a bed against one wall. Suddenly shy, Priya and Bijoy hang back while Rupa explains why she has come. Without speaking, the lady taps some numbers into the machine to break the lock and then passes the receiver to Rupa who hesitates.

She can't do this, the two worlds have always been separate, the woman of Baba's story is not the same woman who works for a care agency in England, and neither of them at this moment is her mother. And what about the children, this telephone brings their thakurma unbearably close, won't they wonder why she doesn't ask to speak to them? The telephone lady shakes the receiver in Rupa's face, her eyebrows raised impatiently. Rupa's fingers fumble in her purse for the piece of paper on which Sunil has jotted down the correct international code.

"It's me, Rupa. How are you?" Although the line is clear it sounds as if she's talking to herself, her voice comes back directly into her own ear. The lady sits down again, folds her arms over her stiffly starched sari and turns her head towards the doorway. Her posture betrays boredom, her expression registers no interest in just one more conversation. Priya tries to catch her eye and soften her with smiles but has no success so looks at the ground in embarrassment. Rupa feels intimidated and switches into English.

"Yes that's right, six o'clock in the morning. There's no need to come to the airport, Ma, unless you want to. If I get the early coach I should be home by lunchtime." The meter ticks away second by second, recording a rapidly increasing sum. Bijoy is jumping up and down the steps, still engrossed in his battle with the rakkhosh.

"What? Say that again. You're planning to go where?" The tone of Rupa's voice alters, both Priya and Bijoy glance up at her face. The thin lady continues to stare blankly through the doorway.

"Yes, of course I'll tell him if you want me to, if you're quite sure. Don't worry. See you soon then, bye." She nods reassuringly at the children and replaces the receiver.

The children have got the hang of the story game and on the way home continue to play it by themselves, with occasional appeals to Rupa to act as referee when one of them considers the other's imagination has become too wild. Walking behind them

Rupa tries not to think about the conversation she's just had with her mother, to keep her thoughts suspended until they get back. Instead she wonders about Miss Featherstone's part in the plot. It must have been her idea to send Ma to England, she must have been responsible. How else could everything have been arranged? In a way then Miss Featherstone had prevented a reconciliation, once Ma was out of India there was no chance, well little chance anyway, that she and Baba would contact each other. So Miss Featherstone had been there at the beginning and at the end, had brought them together and had made sure they would stay apart. And no doubt her motives were good. She thought the marriage would bring them happiness, security, and then when things went wrong she thought they would be better off in different continents. The best of intentions. Making decisions about other people's lives for sound and defensible reasons, it's what Rupa does in her job all the time. Take this child into Care, place that one with his grandparents, remove another from her current foster home. It wasn't easy to be honest about motives though; the welfare of the child was one of many factors – the state of the departmental budget, the need to maintain your status as a professional, personal prejudice. Could you blame Miss Featherstone? That would depend on why she acted as she did.

Priya and Bijoy race the last few hundred yards and dash inside the house to look for their mother, and then tell her, with much excitement and mutual contradiction, the amazing story they've made up. Rupa can see Sunil crouching in the shadows beside his aviary, a solid structure built of bricks and mortar with a tin sheet for roofing, and goes to join him.

"Did you get through alright?" He removes a padlock, opens a mesh door set in the wall and takes out four small aluminium bowls. These he fills with a mixture of soaked maize, peas and wheat, he mixes in a little grit and reaches back into the aviary to replace them in wire rings attached to lengths of bamboo. The birds sidle along the perches but are not startled as they watch his hands move through the familiar routine.

"It wasn't difficult. The line was good, I could hear her clearly. Very expensive though, as you warned it would be."

182

Sunil reaches inside again and brings out an old clay bowl, originally used for sweet curd, empties out the stale water and pours in fresh, adding a few drops of medicine before returning the bowl to its place. Then he takes a small lump of soft dough from a dish on the ground beside him and forms it into a ball, molding it round a wire hook.

"She asked me to say she wants to come here, to come and see you all next year after she retires. It's still only a vague idea, she's hasn't worked out any details yet." Although her mother had in fact told her to speak first to Baba, Rupa thinks that Sunil will make a better messenger. "Will you talk to Baba, see what he thinks?"

Sunil shapes more balls and carefully hangs them at intervals round the wire-mesh panels. A lovebird, colorless in the dim light, claws its way along, stretches its neck sideways and begins to peck one of the mineral-rich tidbits.

"How strange, how extraordinary! As if she knew we'd found the notebook, that Baba had explained." Sunil is talking to himself, incredulous. He looks at Rupa, "Did she know, surely you didn't tell her?"

Rupa shakes her head, "Of course not!" How could she have, in public, on the phone.

"She wants to stay with us here, in this house?" He's beginning to smile.

"She didn't actually say that, but I suppose it's what she meant."

"I'll talk to Baba, see how he feels. He's told us everything, nothing to hide any more, so why not let her come? He might even be pleased. He wouldn't have to do anything, we'll look after her. As far as I'm concerned, and Chhaya will agree, Ma can visit whenever she likes." Sunil secures the padlock and goes over to wash his hands while Rupa works the pump handle. She loves this brother, so generous of heart.

The creaking of the pump brings Nirmal babu to the edge of the veranda, peering into the yard to see who's taking water so late in the evening.

CHAPTER SEVENTEEN

The final packing has an urgency to it which requires full concentration, but Rupa can never manage to give it that. Always at the end of a holiday, a visit to friends, a conference, her mind is too full of what's happened in the preceding days, or wanders off down inconsequential byways, and will not let her get on with the job of clearing up. As if it's reluctant to accept endings. She has collected from the bathroom the half empty bottle of shampoo, squeezed tube of toothpaste, opened packet of washing powder, and bar of soap with one beautifully smooth flat corner where it dropped on the concrete floor with a waxy thud. All these she will leave with Chhaya, and the cleanser, moisturiser, body lotion and other cosmetic bits and pieces she'll give to Priya ... or should they go to Chhaya also?

Something moves outside the room and Rupa looks up to see her sister-in-law climb the stairs, her upper body tilting to one side to balance the weight of the bucket of wet clothes she's carrying. Chhaya unwinds the thick twisted ropes of cloth, the result of strenuous wringing, and shakes out the saris before spreading them over the line so that they hang down heavily against the side of the house. Rupa hasn't spoken to her since relaying Ma's message to Sunil, and wonders whether she should go out now, ask her how she feels about the prospect of a visit from a mother-in-law she's never met. Not an easy adjustment to make.

But remembering how reluctant Chhaya was to discuss the subject last time it was raised, Rupa decides to let her choose the moment. When she's finished hanging the washing surely she will come in to talk, on this the last morning.

After much deliberation Rupa is of the opinion that Ma's wish to visit her family confirms Baba's version of their separation, it suggests she's not guilty of any great sin, otherwise she'd be too ashamed even to think of coming. You could argue, if you wanted to defend the opposite theory, that many years of living in England where affairs are commonplace and unremarkable, have altered Ma's view of what's shameful and what isn't. But Rupa is certain that's not the case. It's only a wish of course, whether her mother will actually come or not Rupa wouldn't like to say, still the intention itself says much.

The thought of seeing her mother again sends Rupa into shivers. How will they behave with one another, negotiate a new relationship, begin to discuss people of whom they have never spoken? Will the process be shy and painful, lasting many days or even weeks, delivered in small measures, or a ceaseless free-flowing revelation fuelled by endless cups of tea and coffee, continuing like Ma's night shifts through to breakfast the next morning? Rupa will assert herself, insist on hearing all there is to hear, she will not be denied this knowledge.

Chhaya has finished with the saris now and is resting one elbow on the wall, her face turned sideways so that Rupa can see her profile. If she doesn't come into the bedroom soon then Rupa will gather up the half-used bathroom things and take them out to her.

Rupa picks up the assorted gifts she's piled on her bed and eases them, one at a time, between the layers of clothing in the suitcase. This should cushion fragile items against breakage. On the other hand if she's asked to unpack at Customs this method could prove hazardous. Perhaps she should retrieve the packets and put them all together in her hand luggage instead? She hesitates, and becomes fascinated with her own hands.

Why do you say you knew something "like the back of your

185

hand" when you mean you know it intimately? She never studies the backs of her hands, as she looks at them now they are strangers to her. Nails, now that's a different matter, displayed on outstretched fingers or folded over towards her, the eight faces are old friends (thumb nails being at an awkward angle have to be viewed separately). Their expressions change according to whether they have just been clipped or have grown into elegantly tapered ovals. Rupa only stopped biting her nails a few years ago, remembers chewing away while sitting her final exams, so now she takes great delight in her carefully manicured hands. One nail has split at the edge, a tiny tear but still enough to catch on the clothes as she handles them. That's what Chhaya has been like these last few days, like a torn nail snagging on everything and everyone she encounters, whereas she's usually filed down to a perfect smoothness. Another movement outside and Rupa looks up expecting to see Chhaya in the doorway, but there is no one, only the saris blocking out the view and already beginning to dry.

"Pishi, Rupa pishi! The taxi's here." Bijoy comes up the stairs moving his feet to an odd rhythm, probably in time with the song which plays in his head. "And Jayanti pishi says you've to leave your suitcase in your room, someone will bring it down in a minute."

Rupa feels the coldness of each concrete stair under her tread, and the roughness of the concrete banister under her sliding palm. She stops for a moment to wink her farewell into the eye of the alert and broody hen. She lingers in the kitchen noticing the debris of their midday meal, a dish of well-chewed and discarded fish bones, yellow splashes on the formica tabletop, before emerging onto the veranda. Priya is huddled moodily on one corner of the iron bed but manages to produce a watery smile for Rupa's sake.

"Stupid girl, she wants to go to school today, the day when you're going away. See, she's put on her uniform all ready to be off. What does she think? She won't be here to say goodbye to her Pishima from England? Utter rubbish! Of course I wouldn't

186

let her go to classes, she has to say goodbye with the rest of us."
Nirmal babu is agitated, sitting in his easy chair but shifting restlessly
from one position to another.

"Listen Priya, I'm a teacher with responsibilities, but even
then I've come back early to say goodbye to your Rupa pishi."
Jayanti is dressed for school and behaves as if she's in charge
of this departure scene.

"I knew that if I stayed I'd be sad and would cry, so I wanted
to go to school and not have to watch you leaving." Priya's face
is a strange combination of misery and mirth, her eyes shine with
a mixture of tears and amusement.

"I'm very glad you stayed at home." Rupa presses Priya's
cheeks between her palms. Turning to Jayanti, "And I knew you,
my only sister, wouldn't miss saying goodbye, school or no school."

As Nirmal babu rises to his feet to pray for Rupa's safety
throughout the forthcoming journey, Jayanti and Chhaya cover
their bowed heads with their saris. Sunil places the suitcase
on the veranda steps and joins the standing circle. Rupa
doesn't close her eyes. She can see Bijoy cross-legged on
the iron bed bending over his school books, tracing with his
finger what he reads, determined to show he's not affected
by the emotion which trembles in his grandfather's voice.
She can see tangled strands of hair covered in dust and fluff
nestling where the red floor meets the wall. She can see her
house-wearing sandals, cheap ones bought from a roadside
stall, which she won't wear in England so is leaving for Chhaya
to give to the old beggar woman who calls in once a month
to complain of the cruel treatment she receives at the hands
of her only son. She can see ... Nirmal babu's prayer
disintegrates completely into shuddering silence and they all
say "Amen." Someone sighs.

"Well then, Baba, I'm leaving," Rupa stoops to take the dust
of his feet and as she straightens up he grips her arm and holds
out a sealed envelope, slightly creased, with no one's name upon
it.

"This is for her, for your mother." His voice has regained its dignity. Rupa takes the letter quietly and pushes it into the outside flap of her hand luggage, trying not to show how she feels, trying not to imagine the exact moment when she hands this letter to her mother. She can sense the letter's glow through the leather flap and has to restrain herself from putting her hand against the spot. Instead she reaches out to grasp her father's hand, he grins widely and returns the pressure.

"Why didn't you tell me that you were going to write? If I'd known I'd have put in a letter of my own." Jayanti is annoyed. And then to Rupa, "Tell her I'll write separately and post it later."

A few neighbors have gathered round the taxi to see her off and they watch as Sunil struggles to force the suitcase into the boot. The boot doesn't close properly and Rupa suggests tying it with string but the driver says not to worry, it'll be fine. Rupa has visions of arriving at Dum Dum airport only to find the boot is empty, her suitcase lying forlornly somewhere along the route. The neighbors smile at Rupa and wish her a safe journey and hope she'll be back again soon. Sunil opens the chrome handled front door and climbs in, stretching his arm out along the top of the seat so that he can easily turn to speak to his youngest sister who sits in the back cradling her hand luggage on her knee.

Nirmal babu has stayed on the veranda and Rupa can see Bijoy eagerly explaining something to him, pointing to the book which he holds up close to his grandfather's face. Chhaya's head is still covered, she lifts a handful of cloth to wipe her eyes. Priya hides her face in her mother's sari and howls, as she predicted she would. Jayanti leans into the taxi and asks Rupa to check that she has put her ticket and passport somewhere easy to get at but safe from pickpockets. Passport and ticket? The envelope containing the letter written by Baba to Ma, that is her priority. As the taxi begins to move, bumping slowly away from the house, Jayanti is left standing by herself.

Customers lounging on the wide step in front of Chhoto kaku's shop turn their heads to look, some of them wave. Further round the corner Haldar babu's wife stands unsmiling in front of her thakur-ghor. Reaching under her sari she scratches her back. Because the lane is so narrow, cyclists have to dismount and wheel their cycles into gateways to let the taxi pass. Pedestrians step backward into hedges. Leaves brush the car doors and appear at the windows. Women pause in their work to watch the vehicle pass. Children come running to peer inside and then chase behind as the taxi gradually increases speed. In the middle of the road someone has made a little shrine, a few flowers, a tiny clay lamp, an incense stick. The driver touches his forehead in a gesture of respect as his taxi passes over.

Cousin Khuku is waiting in the road with some of her neighbors who link arms and laugh and won't let them drive by. They must stop to say goodbye properly.

"So Rupa, you're leaving us. Your holiday's finished. What time's your flight?" Khuku leans on the door and sticks her toothy smile through the open window.

"Eight o'clock this evening unless there's some delay. I should be home by lunchtime tomorrow." Rupa doesn't resist as Khuku takes her hand affectionately. The women crowd round and comment on Rupa's courage, for a young woman to travel so far alone! Doesn't she feel afraid?

"How long does it take then? How long will you have to sit in the plane?" Khuku is speaking extra loud to include her neighbors in the conversation. Rupa dreads what's coming next, another frustrating attempt to explain the concept of time zones. With her free hand she touches Sunil's arm and he, thank goodness, correctly interprets her plea for help.

"I'll explain it to you another time, Khuku. Listen, we've really got to go now or we'll be late. Passengers have to check in long before the plane's due to leave." He nods to the driver who restarts the engine and as they judder forward Rupa waves to cousin Khuku's hollow figure surrounded by women chattering.

"She'll be alright won't she? I mean with her neighbors, they're all Hindu in this area aren't they. Only, when we visited her house, she was talking about what the Pope said, she sounded as though she expected trouble. She joined in a protest march, did you know that?" Rupa feels inexplicably anxious about Khuku who looks suddenly pathetic, despite the grin.

Sunil swivels himself round in surprise. "Khuku? Of course she'll be alright. She gossips, she's excitable, but she's as tough as they come. Lives much more closely with those around her than we do." Confident that he's done enough to reassure his sister, he turns to face the road in front. "Don't worry about her." Both fall silent as they brace themselves against the jolts and bounces of the vehicle's uneven progress.

ABOUT THE AUTHOR

Alison Mukherjee was born in Britain and has lived and worked in India. She obtained a Masters in Theology from Serampore College, West Bengal, and recently completed a Ph. D at the Mission Studies department of Birmingham University. She has taught Religious Studies in schools and colleges, and is currently employed as a qualified social worker. She is married and has three grown-up children. *Nirmal Babu's Bride* is her first novel.